The Binding

D1313365

First published 2015 by
A & C Black, an imprint of Bloomsbury Publishing Plc
50 Bedford Square, London, WC1B 3DP

www.bloomsbury.com

Bloomsbury is a registered trademark of Bloomsbury Publishing Plc

A CIP catalogue for this book is available from the British Library

ISBN 978 1 4729 0872 8

Typeset by Newgen Knowledge Works (P) Ltd., Chennai, India
Printed and bound by CPI Group (UK) Ltd, Croydon CR0 4YY

1 3 5 7 9 10 8 6 4 2

The Binding

Jenny Alexander

A & C BLACK
AN IMPRINT OF BLOOMSBURY
LONDON   NEW DELHI   NEW YORK   SYDNEY

Contents

Part One: Coming to the island

Question: *What's the difference between a teacher and a train?*

Answer: *The teacher says 'Spit your gum out' and the train says 'Chew, chew, chew!'*

Now, what's the difference between what you think it would be like to spend the summer on a tiny Scottish island and what it's really like? Answer. . . Where shall I start?

Chapter 1

The backbone of a jellyfish

'Think about it, Dee,' said Matt. 'It would be amazing!'

Mum actually did seem to be thinking about it. They both pored over his laptop, looking at the pictures. Her idea of a great holiday is somewhere hot with a swimming pool, but Matt was too new to know that yet— he'd only been living with us for a couple of months.

'What?' said Tressa, coming up out of her book like a submarine surfacing. 'What would be amazing?'

'Jean next door has just offered us her cottage on Morna for the whole summer,' Matt said, turning the laptop towards her. 'She can't go this year because of her ankle.'

Tressa shot me a look, like it was my fault Jean fell off her ladder, just because I happened to be holding it at the time. I personally don't think people older than your granny should go up ladders, but she had insisted and I was only trying to help.

'Well it's a stupid idea.' Tressa downed periscope and sank back into her book.

Milo brm-brmmed his ambulance across his car-mat. There had been a horrific pile-up right outside the supermarket, involving about ten cars of all different shapes and sizes.

'I don't think we should dismiss it out of hand,' said Mum, who would definitely have done just that when Dad was around, if it was him who had suggested it. You could tell she was trying to think of a way to get out of it though, without upsetting Matt.

'So you're saying you actually want to go?' scoffed Tressa, surfacing again. 'I don't think so!'

'We're just talking about it, all right?' said Mum.

4

Milo abandoned his medical emergency, picked up Nee-na and sat back on his haunches. Other five-year-olds have cuddly toys but he has a police car with doors that open. It's small enough for him to hold in his fingers while he sucks his thumb, which he isn't supposed to do any more now that he's started school.

'There's a shop on the island,' Matt said, obviously thinking that might be a selling point with Tressa. 'Jean says it stocks everything you could possibly need.'

Tressa glanced at the picture he had brought up on the screen and snorted like an indignant hippo. The kind of shop that stocked everything she needs would have to be a mile-long mall. Milo stuck his thumb in his mouth and watched them over his fist.

While Matt went on trying to convince Mum, with things like 'It's got a library,' and 'The children will love it,' Tressa went on snorting and tossing her hair, and I dropped down onto the floor beside Milo.

'Don't get your knickers in a knot,' I told him. 'We'll just end up staying here as usual.'

We hadn't been away in the summer holidays since Dad moved out to live with Donna, which was three years ago. I didn't mind, though—we had sleepovers and camped in the garden and stuff like that, plus Dad came down several times to take us out for the day. He and Mum don't talk to each other, which is bad, but nowhere near as bad as it used to be when they did.

Milo smiled, and his thumb slipped out. But then. . .

'All right—let's do it!' said Mum.

My eyebrows shot half-way up my forehead and seemed to get stuck. Milo gave me a horrified look. Tressa snapped her book shut.

'Well, you can go, I don't care. But I'm not going!'

For someone who's supposed to be clever, Tressa can be really stupid. I mean, everyone knows that if you're twelve, you can't stay at home while your family goes on holiday. What was she thinking? That she could stay with Dad? In his one-bedroom flat with Donna, who Tressa one hundred per cent hates?

Or did she think she could stay with her friends? Maybe some people could, for a week, but not for the whole summer, and anyway Tressa hasn't really got any friends unless you count Lana and Jodie, and she doesn't seem to like them all that much, except to boss around. She'd much rather spend her time trawling through books, scooping up long words she can use for showing off with, such as 'ingest', which doesn't mean, as you might think, 'only joking' but 'take food into the body', or as any normal person would say, 'eat'.

'Just take a pile of books with you,' I said. 'All you're going to do in the holidays is read anyway, so what difference does it make where we are?'

It was annoying. I mean, sometimes you just have to suck it up. It wasn't as if she'd be missing out on good stuff such as playing footie in the park or swimming at the lido or making rope-swings and zip-wires in your best mate Benjie's back garden (don't tell Mum).

'We'll get to go on two planes and a boat,' said Matt. 'It'll be a real adventure.'

Way to get Milo onside! I actually quite liked the sound of that myself, plus it reminded me of a joke. 'What did the water say to the boat? Nothing—it just waved!'

Tressa jumped up and turned her fire on me.

'Everything's a joke with you. I hate you, Jack!' she said. Then, bang! She flounced out, slamming the door behind her.

I wish that Tressa was a sulker. Then if she didn't get her own way, she'd go off in a huff and everyone could just ignore her. But it's really hard to ignore someone who's in a massive strop. She kept it up for the whole of the rest of term, even after Mum and Matt had got the tickets and there was no way any of us were going to get out of it.

She was furious with Matt for wanting to go, with Mum for caving in and with me for not saying anything. 'If you'd taken my side, they'd have had to listen,' she said. Like that would have made any difference.

She kept it up even when the rest of us started to feel excited.

'Just give it a chance,' said Mum. 'The island really does look beautiful.'

But, see, here's the first difference between how we thought it was going to be and how it was—when we got to the island, it didn't look like Jean's photos at all. Or rather, it did, but only in parts.

On one side of us, as the boat came alongside the jetty, there was a gorgeous white sandy beach, but on the other was a kind of gulley which was full of broken plastic bottles and smashed-up rubbish, with a rusty old cooker on the top.

There were two buildings near the shore, which looked as if they'd once been houses. One seemed to be used as some kind of store, and the other had half its roof missing and all the windows boarded up. There were three rusty wrecks of cars at one end, with all the windows out and grass growing on the seats. The whole place looked as depressed as a goalie who's missed a penalty.

Matt said obviously Jean wouldn't have chosen the tatty bits to take pictures of, but we could do like her, and just focus on the lovely bits.

'Was that a rat?' said Mum, as a streak of brown disappeared in the seaweed bundled up at the top of the beach.

The second difference was that things weren't the way we'd imagined from Jean's descriptions. Most people round where we live, if you say there's a shop that sells everything, would assume you mean a really great shop.

The island shop wasn't a proper shop at all. It was somebody's house, just up from the jetty, and it didn't even have any set opening times—you had to go in and shout.

'The door's always open,' the shopkeeper said. 'No-one locks their doors here.'

She wiped her hands on her apron, which looked as if she'd wiped them on it lots of times before, and stood behind the counter, waiting for us to choose. All the food was behind her, on dark wooden shelves that covered the whole wall, floor to ceiling.

The choice seemed to be things in tins, dried stuff like rice and pasta, long-life milk, and a billion sorts of biscuits, from ordinary ones like cream crackers and bourbons, to oatcakes and something called 'butter biscuits' in plastic bags, which looked as tasty as cardboard.

There were two boxes of eggs on the counter and a sack of potatoes on the floor in front of it, beside a box of carrots and a big bag of onions. While Mum and Matt were getting the food, me, Tressa and Milo started looking through the bashed-up books and board games in a big bookcase behind the door.

'Help yourselves to anything you fancy from the library,' the shopkeeper said. It wasn't exactly the kind of library we had been expecting.

When we'd got everything, someone called Jimmy came to take us up to Jean's house. We put our bags and shopping on the back of his tractor and followed him up there.

When someone says 'tractor' you think of a big, shiny machine that blocks up country lanes, but this one was about the size of a quad bike with a little trailer, and it looked nearly as old and ramshackle as Jimmy. We didn't have to worry about keeping up, as its top speed was snail's-pace, and it kept completely stopping.

In Jean's pictures, the sea and sky were bright blue, and everything seemed to sparkle in the sun, but the day we arrived was all-over grey, and as cold as December. Matt said never mind—it just meant we'd feel all the more cosy in our snug little cottage.

Which brings me to the third big difference between what we imagined it would be like and what we found. Jean's house, which looked white and shiny from a distance in the pictures, when you got close up, looked damp and shabby. Inside, instead of being quaint and historical, everything looked old and out of date.

There was a dog-eared exercise book full of information and instructions about things like how to light the peat fire and where the candles were kept. Yes, candles. Morna didn't have a proper electric supply like everywhere else in the universe, just a generator that came on for a few hours in the evening.

You couldn't use electric kettles or toasters or fan heaters, because they took too much power to run, and the fridge and freezer were in an outbuilding because they went off overnight. There was no mobile connection and the internet was patchy.

Matt said, 'We'll manage for a month. We can get some board games from the shop!' but even he was sounding doubtful now. Milo was the only one who looked happy, and that was because he had spotted a wrecked old van in the field behind the house.

'Can I go out and play?'

'We'll all go and have a look around outside,' Mum said. 'We might as well. It can't be colder than it is in here!' She made it sound like a joke, but if it was Dad instead of Matt who'd brought us to a chilly, tatty place like this, it would have been a full-on massive grumble.

Tressa and me trailed out after them.

'This is your fault,' she hissed. 'You've got the backbone of a jellyfish!'

Not that again! Just because she was always up for a fight.

'What's the point in making a fuss over things you can't change?' I said. 'Anyway, maybe I wanted to come!'

'Yeah, right.'

If I'd known any jellyfish jokes, I'd have said one, to annoy her, but I didn't. I do now though.

What kind of fish goes well with ice cream?

Jellyfish!

Chapter 2

Trespassing

Milo wanted to go straight to the van, so we all walked across the concrete yard, between the sheds and out into the field, which sloped up towards the hill behind the house. It looked like autumn, with brown leaves strewn all over the grass, until you realised there weren't any trees.

What looked like dead leaves turned out to be sheep's droppings. They were everywhere, but then, so were the sheep. They weren't fat and fluffy like sheep are supposed to be, but scrawny and small, with little stick legs and bits of dirty wool trailing under their bellies like rags.

The van had no tyres on one side so it leaned right over, and the driver's side door had fallen open. Grass was growing around the bottom edge, so it was completely stuck. Mum and Matt tried to close it but they couldn't. They went right round the van, pushing and pulling at various bits of it, before deciding it was safe for Milo to play in.

Mum let him stay out there on his own while we did an inspection of the outbuildings, so that Matt could locate the peat store and she could make sure there weren't any hidden dangers, such as open trapdoors or rat poison or ladders. She said that here, on this island in the middle of nowhere, with no traffic and hardly anyone around, it would be perfectly safe for Milo to play outside on his own, once she'd done some basic checks.

'Same goes for you guys,' Matt said to Tressa and me, quickly adding, 'If your mum says so, of course.' He's always dead careful not to act like he thinks he's our dad, ever since Tressa went off on one when he and Mum were talking about him moving in. 'I don't want him here!' she'd yelled. 'He's not my dad!'

Mum smiled and nodded at Matt, then said to us, 'It's impossible to get lost on an island, so feel free to go off and explore.'

Free. I liked the sound of that, and Tressa actually cracked a smile.

We crossed the stony track in front of the house and headed down towards the sea. It was late afternoon by then, and the clouds had lifted. The sun was pale and low in the sky.

It didn't take us long to reach the shore. The cliffs were not high or steep, and we could easily have clambered down onto the strip of rocky beach, but we stood at the top to take in the view.

We could see the mainland, like a thin rumpled ribbon of blue, stretched out along the horizon. Gulls were swooping and gliding low over the water, sometimes dropping suddenly to dive for fish.

'Why do seagulls fly over the sea?' I said. 'Because if they flew over the bay, they'd be bagels!'

Tressa didn't laugh, but she didn't bite my head off either, so things were looking up, strop-wise.

'Which way?'

We decided to go left, in the opposite direction from where the boat came in. Rabbits grazing on the edge of the cliff looked up as we passed, but didn't bother to run away. Sheep continued on their ambling tracks. It felt as if no living person had ever walked there before.

After about ten minutes, we rounded a headland, and suddenly the shore flattened out. The grass sloped gently down onto a wide pebbly ridge, above a beach of white sand with not a footprint on it.

Tressa started running, and I ran after her, all the way down to the water's edge. We played leapfrog and hop-skip-jump, and looked for shells, and we didn't even notice the building until we started back up the beach to go home.

It was huddled under the low cliff at the far end of the beach, where the land began to rise again. We crossed the sand and crunched over the pebbles. At the top of the beach, the stones got bigger and the short grass growing in the gaps looked like water flowing round them. Up by the building, all the stones had been cleared away and there was a small strip of tufty, bright green grass.

The building was long and low, with two small windows, one on each side of the door. When we got closer, we could see that the roof was held down by wires attached to wooden pegs that had been pushed into cracks in the stone walls. There was glass in the windows, all grimy and cobwebby, and the door looked as if it might have once been blue, but the paint was mostly worn away.

Tressa put her hand on the handle.

'We can't go in!' I said. 'That's. . .well, that's. . .'

'Trespassing?'

Trust her to remember the word.

'It's only trespassing if the door's locked,' she said. 'If you don't lock your door, you're just asking for people to come in.'

'What if someone's inside?'

On the upside, she didn't call me a jellyfish, but on the downside, she didn't take any notice of me either. She turned the handle and pushed. The door wasn't locked. We couldn't see anything inside until our eyes got used to the dark, because hardly any daylight could get in through the tiny windows in the thick stone walls.

The floor was bare earth, and there wasn't any ceiling, just rafters under the uneven slates of the roof with, here and there, a few little chinks of daylight blinking through. The walls looked the same inside as outside, just stones with gaps and cracks between.

It was all one room, with a fireplace at one end. There was a pile of driftwood in the hearth. You could tell that someone had been there, and not very long ago.

There were three fish-boxes in the middle of the room, facing in like a ring of chairs, with a table in the middle made of a piece of driftwood balanced on four big stones.

'Look at this,' Tressa said.

She had found a square recess in the wall with a weather-beaten piece of wood rammed into it to make a shelf. On the shelf, there were matches and candles, a plate and a knife, and an unopened packet of digestives. Underneath the shelf there was a tin box that someone had written some words on in white paint.

Privite-keep out.

'That's a child's writing,' Tressa said. 'This is a den!'

She tried to prise the box open, but it was locked.

'Do you suppose they light candles and have fires and everything?' I said, picking up the matches.

In the darkest corners of the room, we found strange circles of things laid out on the floor. There was a ring of shells and another of stones; a ring of buoys and a ring of bones. Lined up along a ridge in the wall at one end, there was a row of fragile little skulls. I asked Tressa what kind of animal she thought they were.

'The beaks might be a clue,' she said. I remembered seeing a dead seagull in a tangle of seaweed and ropes at the other end of the beach.

When we'd had a good look around, we went back outside and stood blinking in the daylight. As we shut the door, we saw someone on the edge of the cliff above, looking down at us. We stepped back a bit, trying to see him better, but the sun was behind him, and all we could make out was a black silhouette. He looked a bit taller than me, but he wasn't skinny, and he was holding a long stick.

'Hi!' I shouted up at him.

Two other figures appeared to his right. They looked like a boy and a girl, but it was difficult to tell as the sinking sun made silhouettes of them too.

'We've found your den,' shouted Tressa.

Without a word, all three of them turned away and disappeared back over the cliff. Tressa made one of her famous snorting noises.

'Weird,' she said. 'It looks like things might just be starting to get interesting!'

Chapter 3

A meeting on the beach

Question: *Why did the pony clear his throat?*

Answer: *Because he was a little hoarse! ('Horse'—get it? A little horse!)*

There were lots of ponies on the grass around the old wrecked van the next morning, when we set off to walk up the hill. Me and Tressa didn't really want to. We'd much rather have gone back to the den, but we didn't say so because then they might all want to come with us. We wanted to keep it secret.

But Matt insisted that the best thing to do, when you're in a new place, is to go to the top of the nearest hill and get the lie of the land. It's probably a geography teacher thing.

'Onwards and upwards!' he said, striding ahead.

You could tell that Milo didn't really want to go either. As we passed the old van, he would've dived into it and stuck like a limpet, if Mum hadn't grabbed his hand and kept him going in the right direction.

We knew from looking at the map that the island was shaped like a teardrop, with a ridge of hills running down the west side like a spine. We trudged across the open moorland towards the highest part of the ridge, and soon we saw a triangulation point on the horizon.

It was a sunny morning but not very warm, because of the wind, which got stronger the higher we climbed. Mum and Milo kept stopping for a rest, so Tressa, Matt and me were the first ones to the top. From there, we could look across the whole of the east side, as it sloped down from the hills and flattened out towards the sea.

We could see the jetty where the boat came in, and the houses dotted around it. Almost all the houses on the island seemed to be in that area, with only ours and a few old wrecks further along the track, and one right at the very end, where the track ran out to the north. Matt looked for it on his map. He said it was called Anderson Ground.

On the west side of the island, the land was rocky and rugged. Matt said there were high cliffs all the way along that side, with no beaches or harbours or houses.

'One day, we should walk all the way round the coast,' he said.

Watching Mum and Milo still struggling up the hill, 'one day' was probably a bit optimistic. You would have to allow at least a week.

Instead of going straight back down, we walked along the ridge to see if we could get a better look at Anderson Ground. The island was completely bare of trees, except for one or two small spindly ones, huddling behind houses or leaning low to the ground, bashed down by the wind, so we were really surprised to see a square plantation of trees nestling in the bottom of the next valley. It looked like a giant's dark green handkerchief dropped down between the hills.

There was a house among the trees, still with its roof on, so maybe somebody lived in it. 'That's also called Anderson Ground,' Matt said, squinting at his map. Considering there were only about fifty houses on the island, you'd have thought they could have thought of enough names without having to use the same one twice.

We walked back to the triangulation point, where Mum and Milo were sitting on some flat rocks having another rest. The sky was blue and the sea, all around us, was sparkling in the sunshine. The island was bigger than we first thought, so there would be plenty of places to explore. It felt like we were sitting on the top of our own little world.

Coming back down took half the time and, when we walked into the house, it felt warm and cosy because Matt had finally got the hang of making a fire with peat. We had beans on toast and straight afterwards Milo fell asleep on the rug in the middle of his cars.

Everyone was in a good mood, until Matt asked me and Tressa to help with the dishes. He said we would all have to pull our weight, since there weren't any modern conveniences such as a dishwasher.

24

Tressa doesn't so much pull her weight as throw it around, and she wasn't having any of it.

'Why should I?' she said. 'I never asked to go back to the Middle Ages!'

At least she didn't hit him with, 'You're not my dad!'

Mum and Matt did that thing where old people tell you what it was like when they were young. They didn't even have hot water to wash up in, let alone a dishwasher, and they got frostbite in their fingers blah blah blah. Soon they were talking to each other more than us, and Tressa walked out. Since no-one else was doing the washing up, I got on and did it myself.

'You're such a pushover,' Tressa said, when we finally set off across the fields to the den.

I shrugged. 'It's no big deal. Why do you have to make everything into an argument?'

We followed the fence down through the field and walked along the edge of the low cliffs. Rounding the headland, we paused to look down across the amazing beach.

We heard them before we saw them. The three kids from yesterday were splashing about in a big pool among the rocks at the far end of the beach. We couldn't go into the den with them watching us, so we went to say hello. They got out of the water as we approached, wrapping their towels around them.

'Hello again! I'm Tressa and this is my brother, Jack,' Tressa said. 'We're staying here for the holidays.'

None of them said anything. They just stood looking at us. The big stocky boy had close-cropped brown hair and pale blue starey eyes. The other boy was about the same height but much skinnier, with sandy-coloured hair.

The girl seemed super shy. She glanced at us out of the corner of her eye, and then quickly looked away. She had white blonde wispy hair down to her shoulders, the tips dripping seawater onto her towel. You couldn't tell which one of them was the oldest.

'Have you ever heard of trespassing?' the big boy said.

So that was his problem.

'We didn't know it was private,' goes Tressa. 'The door wasn't locked.'

'Just because a door isn't locked, that doesn't mean you can go barging into someone else's property.'

'We didn't touch anything,' said Tressa.

I remembered her trying to prise the box open; it

was a good job she hadn't managed to. 'We saw it was a den, so we just assumed it was for all the kids here, like a play-park or something.'

'Well it isn't,' the big boy said. 'And it's not a den. It's a meeting place.'

'When do you meet?' I asked, thinking it might be like Scouts or something.

'It isn't for people like you.'

Tressa was annoyed. 'You don't know anything about us,' she said.

When a conversation starts to feel tricky, the best thing to do is change the subject, and I did.

'It's lucky to have a rock pool big enough to swim in.'

'They made it so school could have swimming lessons,' the girl told me. Her voice was silvery soft, like a whisper.

'What, and they let you swim in it on your own, no grown-ups?' I asked, just so that I could hear that voice again. But she didn't say anything. She turned to the big boy instead.

'You can see where they blocked it off at the end,' he said.

When he pointed it out, we realised that the flat bit at the seaward end of the pool was made of concrete.

Their clothes were piled in three heaps along it, and the big boy's stick was leaning across one of them. It reminded me of a joke.

'What's brown and sticky? A stick!'

I was going to pick the stick up, to make the joke work better, but I decided not to. They looked at me blankly, like they'd had a sense-of-humour bypass or something.

'I can swim twenty lengths,' Tressa said, doing that tricky-conversation-time-to-change-the-subject thing. 'And that's in a proper swimming pool.'

'You couldn't do twenty lengths here,' the big boy retorted. 'I bet you couldn't even get in.'

It did look cold.

'Yes I could—unless that would be trespassing, of course.'

'This is our pool, and it's our bothy,' he said, glancing up the beach towards the den. 'You can only come if you pass the test, and there's no way you could do that.'

A flicker of surprise went across the girl's face, like she'd never heard of this test before.

'Ooh, an initiation,' said Tressa. 'Bring it on!'

If there's one thing I hate, it's games of chicken or dare, which it looked like this was turning into.

'We don't have to share their den if they don't want us to,' I muttered to Tressa, under my breath. 'There are lots of other old buildings here. We could make our own.'

'Well?' said Tressa, taking no notice of me.

The big boy grinned at her. It wasn't a nice grin.

'If you want to join, come to the bothy this time tomorrow, and we'll see if you're as tough as you talk.'

We walked back up the beach.

'They're not very friendly, are they?' I said. 'They didn't even tell us their names. Do we actually want to join their club?'

'Look around you,' said Tressa. 'How else are we going to survive a whole summer up here?'

Chapter 4

The fruits of Morna

I told Tressa I didn't like the idea of doing an initiation. We were walking down to the shop with Mum, Matt and Milo after breakfast the next day, to get some board games and buy some tins of fruit. Mum said we couldn't live on rice and pasta the whole holiday or we'd get scurvy.

We were keeping our voices down and hanging back a little, so the others couldn't hear what we were talking about. If Mum heard the word 'initiation' she would freak out.

'They're just making a point,' Tressa said. 'They're cross with us for going into their den.'

'I don't even know if I like them though,' I said, remembering those pale blue eyes, staring us down.

'Once we're in, they'll be much friendlier, you'll see.'

Matt was right about the whole lie-of-the-land thing. Now we'd seen from the top of the hill that almost all the houses on the island were scattered over the flat area round the jetty they felt more interesting somehow, and we were more curious to know who lived in them.

We said hello to a woman hanging out her washing, and had a short chat with a man pushing a wheelbarrow. We saw a few other people in their gardens who waved. They all seemed really nice, but really old.

The track carried on along the top of the beach where the boat came in, so we walked on a little way instead of turning off down to the shop and the jetty. There was a big building at the end which the map said was a hotel. We couldn't see it properly because it was surrounded by a high stone wall, but we found a kind of window with rusty iron bars across it, so we managed to get a glimpse of the garden.

It looked like one of those gardens you go to with your gran and grandpa, where they have a tea-shop with cakes. All tidy lawns and fancy flower-beds.

It felt out of place, like a bright parrot that had taken a wrong turning on its way to Africa and landed on a chilly little rock.

Anyway, the point is, we did a lot of walking that morning, so by the time we'd called in at the shop and been down to the jetty to see if we could see any fish or crabs, Milo should have been too tired to want to come out with Tressa and me after lunch. It never occurred to either of us that we might have to take him with us to the den.

But he was determined and we couldn't really say why we didn't want him to come. We wouldn't have minded normally because though he's much younger than us he can be quite funny.

'I'm not bringing him back if he gets tired,' Tressa said.

'Just don't go too far.' Matt ruffled Milo's hair. 'Then he'll be fine.'

'I won't get tired,' said Milo, jumping up and down on the spot to prove it.

He bounded ahead of us down to the sea, and along the top of the low cliffs, keeping well away from the edge like we told him to. When he saw the beach, he raced down onto the sand, just like we had done on the first day. Then he suddenly stopped.

The children were already there, sitting on the grass outside the den. We caught up with Milo and all walked up the beach together. The girl looked worried and I smiled to try and cheer her up, but she didn't smile back. Maybe she was just one of those people who always look worried.

'This is our brother, Milo.'

The girl said to the big boy, in her whispery voice, 'Isn't he too young? He looks the same age as Meggie and Christa.'

'Who are Meggie and Christa?' I said.

'Meggie's my little sister, and Christa's in year one. They don't come to the bothy.'

The big boy shushed her with a look and said to Tressa, 'Are you sure you want to take the test? It can be dangerous.'

'If you've all done it, I'm sure we can.'

He gestured us to sit down. The other boy went into the den and came back with a piece of wood, shutting the door after him. It looked like the side of a fish-box, with foreign words stamped on it. He placed it on the grass between us.

The big boy took three berries out of his pocket and put them on it. They were small, round and black.

'These are the fruits of Morna,' he said. 'They don't grow anywhere else in the world.'

'Are they poison?' asked Milo.

'They can be,' the big boy said.

'What do you mean?' said Tressa. 'Either they are or they aren't.'

'Well, now, that's where you're wrong. The fruits of Morna take different people in different ways. If one person eats one, it might make them really sick, but if someone else eats one they might just have horrible nightmares instead. Some people's tongues might swell up and go black. But there's always a chance you might not get any bad effects at all. It's down to luck.'

'Are you telling us we've got to eat them?' asked Tressa. He said yes, that was the initiation: we had to eat one each.

Without hesitation, Tressa picked one up and put it in her mouth. She looked at me. I noticed that the girl wasn't looking so scared any more; when the boy had got the berries out, she had actually seemed relieved. So I was pretty sure it was a trick, and I'd have taken one too if Tressa hadn't suddenly scooped up the other two and popped them in her mouth.

'There,' she said. 'I've done it for all of us. Now, let's go in.'

But the big boy didn't move.

'The fruits of Morna can take twenty-four hours to work,' he told her. 'The test will not be over until tomorrow afternoon. By then, you might not want to join.' He got up. 'By then,' he added, 'you might not be able to.' With that, he led the others into the den and shut the door.

Tressa was cross. It wasn't fair making us do a test and then not letting us have the prize. I was fed up with Tressa for eating mine as if, just because I didn't grab it quick like her, I wasn't going to do it at all. Neither of us had thought about what Milo would make of it.

'You ate poison berries,' he said.

'No, I didn't. The boy was just playing a trick.'

'How do you know?' said Milo. 'What if it's real?'

'Look, don't worry,' I said. 'It's. . .a game, that's all. They told us about it when we met them yesterday, so we know it's just pretend.' Sometimes, it's all right to tell a little white lie.

'So can we eat those berries if we see some on the way back?'

Tressa and me looked at each other. We told him no; he should still always check with Mum.

'Are you going to check with Mum tonight, about the ones you've already eaten then?'

If Mum found out that Tressa had eaten some berries when she had no idea what they were, let alone that she'd done it in front of Milo, Tressa would be in major big trouble.

'Of course!' she said. 'I'll check with Mum, so you don't need to say anything.'

We both thought the berries must be OK. I mean, people don't go around poisoning each other, do they? But you couldn't help wondering what they were, and I for one was wishing a bit, by tea-time, that Tressa hadn't eaten them.

When Mum served up a crumble for pudding made with tinned blackberries and apples, I had an idea. I asked her if blackberries grew in Morna. She said she thought blackberries grew in every part of Britain, and there were bound to be brambles growing in gardens and sheltered spots on the island, though they wouldn't be fruiting yet.

'What about other kinds of berries?' I asked, in a general sort of way.

'Little round ones,' Milo said, looking up from his game. He'd already got down from the table and I didn't think he would be listening. When he's playing with his cars you could tell him there was a tiger in the garden, or a massive Easter egg full of jelly babies (which he loves), and he wouldn't even hear you. 'Little round black ones,' he added.

'We saw some on a bush,' Tressa said, quickly.

'Oh, that'll be blueberries,' said Matt, gathering the plates. 'They grow all over the Highlands and Islands.'

'What, not just in Morna, then?'

'No.'

'And are there any berries that do just grow here and nowhere else?'

'That's a funny question!'

It was time for a quick subject-change.

'I know another funny question,' I said. 'What's the difference between a flea and a wolf? One prowls on the hairy and the other howls on the prairie!'

Matt laughed. Tressa managed a smile. Milo said he didn't get it. He listened patiently while Mum explained, frowned as if he was thinking about it, and then asked, 'Are those little round black berries poison?'

'No, no—they're edible, and very tasty too,' said Matt. 'Who'd like a hot drink?'

You would have expected Tressa to be really angry with the big boy, but she wasn't. She thought it was a brilliant trick because although you could be pretty sure the berries couldn't really be poisonous, still you couldn't help wondering, 'What if?'

'That was genius,' she said. 'Now I can't wait to tell him about all the horrible effects I've suffered. That'll put the wind up him!'

Chapter 5

A new moon is a magic moon

'So you've come back then,' the big boy said, when we arrived at the bothy the next day.

'We nearly didn't make it,' Tressa told him, doing her best to look off-colour. 'I had a bad reaction, like you said. I was up half the night being sick.'

The boy gave her a steady look.

'I don't suppose you'll want to join now, in that case.'

I couldn't tell whether he believed her or was just playing along. Milo looked confused. It was the first he'd heard that Tressa had been sick.

'But Matt said. . .'

Tressa talked over him. 'Of course we want to join,' she said. 'The whole point about an initiation is that it's supposed to be tough.'

The boy slowly nodded his head. Tressa said that since we were going to join now, maybe they should tell us their names.

'In the outside world, I'm Duncan, and this is Hamish and Elspeth. But inside the bothy we have different names.'

He nodded to the others and they both got up and went inside. He stayed sitting there, so we stayed too, waiting to see what would happen next. You could tell he didn't feel like talking because he stared straight out to sea and completely ignored us.

What were they doing in there? It seemed to take forever. Tressa glanced at me a few times, rolling her eyes. Milo shuffled across to the edge of the grass on his bottom and started digging around in the stones.

After about a thousand years, Hamish and Elspeth came back out and told Duncan they were ready. They stood aside to let Duncan go in first, then followed straight after him leaving us to bring up the rear.

When we'd been in the bothy before, it had been dark and gloomy, and we had been trespassing. We had thought it was just an old fisherman's house some kids had been using as a den. Now, as we went in, it didn't feel like a den at all. Our mouths fell open in surprise.

Hamish and Elspeth had put tea-lights on the floor all around the edge of the room, and their flickering yellow flames lit up the bottom of the rough stone walls. In the middle of the room, instead of three upturned fish-boxes, there were now six, and they made a proper circle around the makeshift table, on which someone had put the tin box marked *Privite*.

Hamish shut the door, and we sat down where Duncan told us to. We couldn't see each other's faces very well because the candles were behind us. Milo was so excited he couldn't sit still. You could tell he was slightly scared too, because he kept putting his thumb in his mouth and then remembering it made him look like a baby and taking it out again.

Duncan took a small silver key out of his pocket and gave it to Elspeth. She leaned forward and opened the box. On the top, was a piece of black cloth, folded in a square, which she lifted out carefully and laid on one side. Then she brought out a thick stubby candle and a black candle holder shaped like a saucer with a handle.

Hamish got up, fetched some matches from the shelf, lit the candle, and went back to his place. Everything they did felt like a dance, as if they knew all the steps by heart.

The big candle in the middle lit up our faces so that we could see each other better, but the soft light and dark shadows made us look different somehow, and not like ourselves. Tressa's eyes looked wider than normal, and they gleamed intently.

'We are here to accept three new members,' said Duncan, 'into this secret society known as the Binding.'

Elspeth took a silver pen from the box, and a pile of clean paper. Then, lifting it carefully like something precious and fragile, she brought out a small, flat parcel. She unfolded the brown paper to reveal what was inside. Pieces of paper, all the same size, covered with writing.

'Tell them first,' said Duncan, 'the names by which we are known.'

Elspeth pushed her pale hair back behind her ears. She selected a page from her parcel of papers, and read in her whispery voice.

'First, the Lawmaker, who makes the laws we live by. Second, the Deputy. Third the Teller, who writes it all down.'

She put the paper back on the pile. It wasn't exactly hard to guess who was who.

'Now read them the laws,' said Duncan.

Elspeth selected another page.

'These are the laws,' she said. 'They are given by the Lawmaker, and written down by the Teller. One: it is forbidden to tell anyone anything about the business of the Binding. Two: it is the sacred duty of us all to inform on anyone who does tell the secrets of the Binding.'

Elspeth paused, to give us time to take it in. Then she pushed her hair back behind her ears again and carried on.

'Three: the members of the Binding will attend all meetings called by the Lawmaker, and do whatever he tells them to do. Four: anyone who disobeys the Lawmaker must accept the punishment.'

She put the paper down. I caught Tressa's eye. As a world-class bossy-boots, she'd definitely met her match in Duncan.

'What is the punishment?' she asked.

'Whatever the Lawmaker decides,' said Hamish. He pointed to the black cloth. 'This is called the Judgement. The Lawmaker puts it on when he makes up the punishment.'

'What's on the rest of those pieces of paper?' I asked.

Elspeth started to leaf through them.

'The secret past of the Binding. . . The secret places of Morna. . . Two simple rules about how to behave at home. . .'

Tressa interrupted her.

'Can you read us some of them?'

'There isn't time this evening,' Duncan told her. 'If you accept the laws of the Binding, we have to perform your naming ceremony.'

Whatever we thought of the laws, we didn't want to miss the ceremony, so we all agreed.

'Then, Teller—write it down.'

Elspeth got a fresh sheet of paper and wrote on it with the silver pen, 'The names of the new members.'

'Stand up, Milo,' Duncan said.

Milo stood up.

'I name you the Page.'

'Is that because you can read him like a book?' I said, quick as a flash. When a joke pops into your head, sometimes you just can't help yourself.

'No,' Duncan said, as if it was a serious question. 'A page is a young boy, about seven or eight years old, who serves a master in exchange for learning the skills of a knight. It's from the Middle Ages.'

'I didn't know that!' Tressa remarked. Which wasn't something you heard her say very often.

Duncan looked pleased. Then he told Milo he would have some important duties as the Page, such as opening and closing the door for the Lawmaker. Milo was well happy with that. Pages were supposed to be seven or eight, but Duncan had said he could be one, and he was only five!

'Now sit down, Page, and stand up Jack,' said Duncan.

Milo sat down and I stood up, but Duncan didn't say anything straight away. He was so good at this. He made it feel solemn and real.

'I name you the Joker. You will bring more fun into the Binding, not just by telling jokes, but also by organising games.'

That took the wind out of my sails. No-one had ever actually asked me to tell jokes before. Whenever I hit my stride jokes-wise, nearly everyone tells me to go away.

'How do you tease fruit?' I said. 'Bana-na-na-na-na!'

Hamish grinned, Tressa rolled her eyes and Milo said he didn't get it. Elspeth smiled as if she was far away and thinking of something else. Duncan smiled with his mouth, but his blue eyes didn't flicker. They were going to be a tough crowd, but the thing about jokes is you have to wear people down.

'So, sit down, Joker and stand up, Tressa,' said Duncan. 'I name you the Teacher. You called the test an "initiation" and that is a better word. You will share your knowledge here in the Binding.'

How did he know that was the perfect thing to choose for Tressa? She was beaming as she sat back down.

'What about Nee-na?' Milo piped up. 'What's his special name?'

Duncan looked at the little police car in Milo's outstretched palm. It gleamed in the flickering candlelight.

'This is not a place for toys. Don't bring that here again.'

He was spot on with Tressa but he didn't have the measure of Nee-na at all. Nee-na goes everywhere with Milo, including to bed. Sometimes Milo wakes up with a little car-print on his cheek from where he's fallen asleep on him.

'Teller—read what you have written back to us, so that we can agree it's correct.'

Elspeth read what she had written and then passed the paper round, with the pen, and we signed our names at the bottom to show we agreed. Then she parcelled up all the sheets of paper and put them back in the box.

Her hands moved delicately in the candlelight, like little birds fluttering from one thing to another. Her pale hair fell over her face as she worked, wispy and gold. The girls at home were loud and giggly, or sporty, or pink and girly. But Elspeth was a different kind of girl altogether, like someone hardly there, a trick of the candlelight.

Hamish blew out the big candle, and our faces were plunged into the shadows again. Elspeth put the candle and its holder carefully into the box with the parcel of papers, the clean sheets and the silver pen. She put the cloth they called the Judgement in beside it, closed the lid, locked the box and gave the key back to Duncan.

Then they stood up, so we stood up too, and we all joined hands in a circle round the makeshift table, with the locked box in the middle. The circle started turning slowly. As we moved to the left, Duncan said some words, and then, changing direction, we all repeated them.

> *In the winding, round and round*
> *What we wind can't be unwound*
> *What we bind can't be unbound*
> *The Binding*

Duncan said, 'We'll meet here tomorrow at seven o'clock to record the history of the new members and reveal some more of the mysteries.'

'But that's after tea,' I said. 'Our mum will want to know where we're going.'

'Evenings are the best time for histories.' Duncan got up to go. He went towards the door, but then stopped. 'Where is my Page?' Milo dived past him and opened the door, looking delighted with himself.

We came out into the daylight. The sea was glassy and still. Elspeth looked up at the sky and following her gaze, we saw a thin white sliver of moon. I never knew you could see the moon before the sun went down. I'd certainly never noticed that in London. Maybe it only happened here.

'A new moon is a magic moon,' Elspeth said, in her whispery voice. 'That's what my granny used to say. A new moon is a new beginning.'

'Yes, but your granny was a bit mad, wasn't she?' Hamish said, heading off to catch up with Duncan.

All the way back, Milo trotted ahead like a dog on his favourite walk, but when he got to the bent-over tree in front of the house, he turned to wait for us.

'I will have to tell the Lawmaker,' he told me, puffing out his chest. 'You talked to Mum and Matt about the berries.'

I didn't argue, and Milo disappeared into the house.

'This should be good,' Tressa said. 'We're going to see the Lawmaker in action. I can't wait!'

Chapter 6

The eyes and ears of the Lawmaker

Question: *What's the difference between Father Christmas and a warm dog?*

Answer: *Father Christmas wears a whole suit, a warm dog just pants!*

Mum was fussing over Milo, making him put his coat on. You could tell she wasn't happy about us all going out after tea, but Matt said what harm could we come to?

'All right,' she said to me and Tressa. 'Look after Milo and be home by half past eight.'

It had felt like a long day. All I could think about was the Binding, but Tressa and Milo didn't say a word about it in front of Mum and Matt, so I didn't either, and the more we didn't talk about it, the more I seemed to think about it.

'So you're going to meet some island children you've made friends with?' Mum said, tugging at Milo's coat zip. 'And they're about the same age as you?'

'Yes,' said Tressa.

'And you're going to one of their houses?'

Tressa said we were meeting them at the beach, but we'd be back way before dark, so it was just the same as going out in the daytime really.

As we walked down across the grass towards the shore, we all agreed that it had been OK to tell Mum and Matt we'd made friends, because we basically had to, and we hadn't given anything away.

By the time we got to the beach, the bothy was in deep shadow under the low cliff, and they were sitting on the grass outside, waiting for us. Wisps of smoke were rising up from the chimney into the still air.

Duncan asked the Page to open the door for us, wait until we were all inside, and then come in, closing the door behind him. Milo followed his instructions, and when Duncan thanked him, he wriggled like a puppy, all waggy with pride.

The room was set out differently. The upturned fish-boxes were arranged in a semi-circle around the fireplace, where a bright fire of driftwood crackled in the hearth. There were candles placed on jutting-out stones in the wall all around it, and with all the light at one end, the other end of the bothy looked even more shadowy and dark.

The makeshift table was in front of Elspeth, to the left-hand side of the hearth, and Duncan sat opposite her on the right-hand side. He gave her the key and she unlocked the box. Then she delicately took out the black square of cloth they called the Judgement, and the big candle.

She put the candle in its candle-holder, and Hamish lit it. We didn't need it in order to see each other's faces because they were lit up by the fire. It was just the dance.

We waited for Duncan to say something. To our surprise, he looked at Milo and asked him, 'Have you brought Nee-na?' Milo nodded into his chest.

'Then go outside and stay there until I call you back in, and when you come back inside, don't bring him with you.'

I caught Tressa's eye.

'What if he wanders off?' I said. 'We're supposed to be looking after him.'

Duncan fixed Milo with his pale piercing eyes and said, 'He will not wander off. He will stay on the grass right in front of the bothy.'

Milo's bottom lip quivered and his hand moved to put his thumb in his mouth, but he didn't.

'B-but what if the seagulls take him?'

'I told you not to bring him to the bothy,' Duncan said.

Milo went outside, shutting the door quietly after him. We sat there, looking at each other. I listened for the sound of him crying, but the only sounds were the crackle of the fire and the murmur of the sea.

After a few minutes, Duncan called Milo back in.

'Have you left Nee-na outside?'

Milo said, 'Yes.' It was weird, because he didn't look upset or cross—he just looked completely in awe of Duncan.

'Then you can take your place.'

When Milo was sitting down again, Duncan told Elspeth to start a new document. She took a clean sheet from her pile of papers.

'You will call it, "The history of the new members,"' Duncan said.

She wrote it down.

'Now, I'll ask them some questions, we'll listen to their answers, and I will tell you what to write.'

He started with Milo.

'Where have you come from, Page?'

'London,' said Milo.

'What kind of place is London?'

Milo immediately thought of all the things he loved about London. 'It's got cars, all sorts of cars. They're parked in all the roads round us, and you can tell what sort they are by their badges.'

Duncan nodded encouragement and Milo went on.

'It's got buses too, and ambulances and police cars. . .' He glanced wistfully at the door.

'And what else?' said Duncan.

'Trains and planes, lots of planes. . . And the tube!'

'So the places you roam with the Joker and the Teacher are streets and stations?' asked Duncan.

'We don't roam!' Milo looked surprised.

'Why not?'

'Because of bad people and getting lost and. . .and things.'

Duncan said to Elspeth, 'Teller, write this down—
"They came from a city choked with noise and fumes.
It was a dangerous place full of bad people."'

While she wrote it down, Duncan turned to me.

'Joker, tell us, why did you come?'

'Well, me and Milo were in the back garden building
a summer-house. . .' I paused, expecting Tressa to butt
in and tell him it wasn't much of a summer-house
considering it was made of four poles and a sheet, and it
kept falling down, but she didn't. So I carried on.

'We heard Jean from next door calling us from the
other side of the hedge. We couldn't ignore her, so we
crawled through the gap to see what she wanted.'

'Is that the same Jean who owns the house you're
staying in? She lives next door to you in London?'
asked Hamish.

I nodded.

'We call her the birdwoman,' Elspeth whispered.
'She comes up every year and just sits on the cliff with
her binoculars.'

That made sense; my story was to do with birds
too—the birds in Jean's garden.

'She said the woodpecker had taken some of the
chicks from her bird box, and she was trying to make

55

it woodpecker-proof. The problem was, the ladder kept wobbling, probably because she's a bit wobbly herself, so she wanted someone to hold it steady.'

'Which was me and Jack,' Milo said.

'And what a great job you did,' said Tressa, rolling her eyes.

'Who's telling this story?' I glared at Tressa. 'Anyway, the ladder suddenly tilted when Jean was half way up, and I thought she was going to land on Milo, so I made a grab for her and she landed on me instead.

'She felt so bad about it that she offered us her house up here for the summer, considering she couldn't come herself, what with a broken ankle and everything.'

Duncan told Elspeth to write, 'The birdwoman fell from a tree and gave them the key to her house in Morna.' Then, while she was writing it, he asked Tressa, 'What did you expect to find here?'

Tressa said, to be honest, she thought it was going to be really boring. 'I was dreading it—no offense!'

'"They didn't know what they would find here." Write that,' Duncan told Elspeth. '"They were ignorant and afraid."'

When she had finished writing, Duncan asked her to read the whole thing back.

'The history of the new members,' Elspeth read. 'They came from a city choked with noise and fumes. It was a dangerous place full of bad people. The birdwoman fell from a tree and gave them the key to her house in Morna. They didn't know what they would find here. They were ignorant and afraid.'

She gave the paper and pen to Tressa for her to sign and pass on so that we could all sign it to show we agreed it was true.

'But this makes London sound horrible,' Tressa said, her pen hovering above the paper.

'So London isn't full of traffic noise and pollution?' asked Duncan. 'It's perfectly safe to roam around on your own? You feel everyone is nice?'

'Well. . .' goes Tressa. 'It's not true we were ignorant and afraid!'

'You said you thought it would be boring here,' said Duncan. 'Are you bored?'

Tressa frowned.

Duncan said, 'You told us you were dreading it. You're the one who knows all the words. Doesn't dread mean fear?'

Tressa shrugged and signed the paper. She passed it to me and I signed it before passing it on to Milo.

'Now you've heard our history, could we hear the history of the Binding?' I asked.

Duncan nodded to Elspeth, who sorted through her papers and took one out. She read it to us.

'The secret history of the Binding. In the beginning, there were four. Duncan Fairfax was the Lawmaker, Hamish McFee was the Deputy, Elspeth Anderson was the Teller and Fin Anderson was the Warrior. They found the bothy and made it into a secret place. The Lawmaker made up the name and the ceremonies of the Binding, and the Teller wrote them down.'

'Who's Fin?' asked Tressa. 'Why isn't he here?'

Hamish said Fin was short for Finlay. 'Finlay Anderson was Elspeth's cousin. He moved away when his dad got a job on the mainland last year.'

'Why did you need a warrior?' I had to ask, I couldn't help it. I mean, maybe there was a rival gang on Morna, and you don't want to get involved in anything like that.

'We didn't,' said Duncan.

Elspeth looked as if she was going to say something, but changed her mind. No wonder she always seemed so serious. She must be missing her cousin. They all must be missing him, considering how few people there were on the island. I was glad Duncan had named me the Joker, because I wanted to do my very best to cheer them up.

Milo suddenly put up his hand and cried, 'I want to tell on someone!'

'Then we have to make the circle,' Duncan said, standing up. We all put our fish-boxes back in the middle of the room where they were before, and Hamish moved the table. We sat down and watched as Elspeth brought the box, the pen and papers, and the Judgement, and Hamish brought the big candle.

Away from the fire, it felt suddenly colder and darker, although we could still hear the wood crackling in the flames.

Hamish said to Milo, 'If you want to tell on someone, you have to stand up and say, "I am the eyes and ears of the Lawmaker, and I wish to make a report."'

Milo stood up and repeated it carefully.

'What is your report?' asked Duncan.

Seeing his face, Milo wavered, but it was too late to change his mind.

'Jack asked Mum about the berries—I mean, the fruits of Morna—and Matt said they were blueberries. . .and we had some today for tea!'

Hamish jumped up, picked up the black cloth of Judgement, and handed it to Duncan. Duncan slowly unfolded it and placed it on his head. He stood up, and gestured to everyone else to stand as well. He told me to stay where I was. Then he took a step back. One by one, they all copied him, until I was standing on my own in the middle. It was a horrible feeling, like I'd stepped off the edge of a cliff, with them looking down at me from the top.

'Is this true, Joker?'

I nodded.

'We judge,' said Duncan, solemnly, 'that the Joker is guilty of talking about the secret business of the Binding outside the bothy. But because he did not know, at that time, about the Law of Secrecy, he will not be punished.'

He took off the black square of Judgement.

'Now we reward the eyes and ears with gold.'

Elspeth took a pencil-tin out of the box and passed it to Duncan. It was full of little chocolate bars. He gave one to Milo and we all sat down again. We watched as Hamish blew out the big candle, and Elspeth carefully placed all the objects back inside the box, locked it and handed Duncan the key.

'Now that we've named the new members, we should have a celebration,' he said. 'Come back to the beach at the same time tomorrow, and wear warm clothes.'

Wear warm clothes? Couldn't we have a fire again? I felt disappointed.

'Joker, we will ask you for a game,' Duncan said, standing up. We all stood up. The flickering tea-lights in the fireplace wall and the yellow flames of the fire meant we cast long shadows on the floor. We joined hands and walked slowly, one way and then the other, repeating after Duncan:

> *In the winding, round and round*
> *What we wind can't be unwound*
> *What we bind can't be unbound*
> *The Binding*

Outside, the sun had gone and the sky was streaked with red. We set off together up the beach. Milo was happy because the seagulls hadn't taken Nee-na, and now he had a chocolate bar as well.

Tressa asked Duncan if he had made up all the rituals himself.

'We call them ceremonies,' he said. 'But rituals is better. Is there a difference?'

Tressa said she thought the things they did every time they met, such as the key and the box and the candle, were rituals, and maybe ceremonies were more the things they did in a one-off kind of way for special occasions.

'I like that,' said Duncan. 'I chose the right name for you at the naming ceremony.'

Milo needed a pee, and me and Elspeth waited for him while the others went on ahead. We stood there, looking out to sea, listening to him clattering across the stones to find a private place.

'That was quite a story he made up, about our history, with the birdwoman falling out the tree and everything,' I said.

Elspeth said sometimes, in the winter, they would light a fire in the bothy and all sit round, and Duncan would tell stories about his ancestors in Ireland. One of them became the first king of Morna; he crossed the sea from Ireland and rode across the battlefield at Mannon Moor on a magnificent white charger, up to its knees in blood.

'Did Morna really have a king?' I asked. 'Is any of it true?'

Elspeth shrugged.

'I don't suppose it really matters,' I said. 'I mean, he's so clever, you want to hear everything he has to say.'

She didn't answer, so I turned to look at her. She kept gazing out to sea. Her hair looked almost white against the dark cliff.

'Duncan's all right so long as you don't cross him,' she said, in her whispery voice.

I laughed. 'I've got a sister like that.'

'I don't think so,' said Elspeth.

Chapter 7

Six candles

I soooooo wanted to tell Mum about the Binding! It didn't help that, when we told her we were going out after tea again the next day, she got all curious.

'You must invite your new friends over. We'd love to meet them!'

Tressa said, 'No-one goes to each other's houses here. They don't need to. They can go wherever they like.'

'It reminds me of when I was a boy,' said Matt, going all wistful. 'We used to play out all hours, and I don't think I ever brought anyone home for tea.'

'Still,' goes Mum, 'it feels a bit strange not even knowing who these children are.'

Matt said it was different on an island, like stepping back in time to a simpler way of life, when children could have more freedom to roam and families more time to sit around, chat to each other and play games.

Thinking about games, I remembered Duncan wanted me to organise one for the celebration. But what games could you play in a small space by candlelight? The only ones I could think of were animal-vegetable-mineral and charades, and I couldn't imagine Duncan, Hamish and Elspeth playing either of them.

I went outside to do some bounce-and-catch with my tennis ball against the wall. It's surprising how that can help you think of good ideas. Benjie and me were playing bounce-and-catch when we had the idea of making a wet slide down the slope at the bottom of his garden with the plastic groundsheet out of his old tent.

Maybe it doesn't work so well if it's only one person bouncing-and-catching, because by the time we set off for the bothy I still hadn't come up with a single idea.

'Have you left Nee-na at home?' Tressa asked Milo. He nodded.

'Really?' Tressa patted his pockets. 'Wow. He has!'

'Duncan said we can't take toys,' Milo said. 'Jack's going to be in trouble, because look what he's got!'

He pointed at the bulging pocket of my jeans. I'd totally forgotten the tennis ball.

'I'm going to tell on you!' Milo said, obviously scenting chocolate.

'I think someone has forgotten that the Lawmaker asked me to organise a game,' I said. And then I thought, *That's it! We can play some kind of ball-game.*

But how would that work with all those candles everywhere? I was still pondering it when we came to the beach.

We were expecting to see them on the grass outside the bothy, like before. But the door was wide open, and we could hear them crashing around inside. We heard Duncan yell, 'Grab him!' and then some laughing, and then a clatter that sounded like one of the fish-boxes getting knocked over.

We ran to see what was going on, and there was Duncan, framed by the doorway, looking flushed. His blue eyes were glittery bright, and in his hand he had a small bird. It looked frozen with fear.

'We got him,' Duncan said, seeing us outside the door. 'He flew into the bothy and couldn't find his way back out.'

He stepped out onto the grass and opened his hand, and the little bird tumbled down to the ground. It took a few hops, then flapped its wings and flew unsteadily away over the stones.

Duncan stayed outside with us while Hamish and Elspeth prepared the bothy, and when they were ready Milo opened the door for us all to go in. There was no fire in the hearth, just a row of flickering candles along the bottom of the fireplace-wall, leaving the other end of the room in darkness.

How did Hamish and Elspeth decide where to put the candles and how to lay out the room? Duncan must have told them before we arrived. We sat down in our usual places and Duncan gave Elspeth the key. She opened the box and took out the Judgement and the candle. Hamish lit it, and our faces were bathed in soft yellow light.

Elspeth took the parcel of papers and the silver pen out of the box, using exactly the same delicate movements as she had before. Everything was perfect, which made me feel even worse about the part I had to play because, considering I still hadn't decided on a game, that was definitely not going to be perfect.

'This is a celebration,' Duncan said. 'But before we begin, I was thinking the new members might be having a problem keeping the law of secrecy.'

How did he know? It was as if his sharp blue eyes could see right into my mind.

'This is a difficult law to keep, but we have several other laws which will help. So, Teller—read them "Two simple rules about how to behave at home."'

Elspeth opened the packet of papers, looked through them and took one out.

'Two simple rules about how to behave at home. One, always be polite to your parents and do what you're told. Two, never argue with each other when your parents are around.'

Tressa said it wasn't our parents at home. Matt was Mum's boyfriend and he was not, no way, never our dad.

'If he lives with your mum then he counts as a parent,' said Duncan.

Tressa looked like she might explode, but he took no notice. I was thinking, *How is that going to help with the secrecy thing?* He read my mind again.

'You might not think that these two rules will make it easier to keep the law of secrecy,' he went on, 'but try them and you will see.'

We didn't have a chance to discuss it any more because Duncan said it was time for the celebration, and we were going to have it on the beach. Problem solved! On the beach, we could play French cricket.

Milo opened the door and we all filed out, first Duncan, then Hamish, then Elspeth and Tressa and me. I grabbed a long piece of driftwood from the pile behind the bothy for a bat, and caught up with the rest of them down by the water's edge.

The tide was right out, so we had a wide area of firm sand to play on. It reminded me of a joke.

'Why was the sand wet? Because the sea-weed!'

They didn't get it, so I had to explain. They still didn't get it. They didn't know how to play French cricket either, but it's easy to learn and they soon got the hang of it. I thought maybe I might even get them playing football some time—it felt like ages since my last kick-around with Benjie and the boys from school.

When we felt tired, we went up the beach to sit down, where the sand was soft and dry. I found a plastic bottle washed up among the seaweed and put it on a flat rock a little way away. Then we played five-stones-each, taking turns to throw a stone at it and trying to knock it off. They'd never played that either. It was a good job they had me!

The sun had dipped behind the cliffs by then, and the sky was getting darker. Duncan looked at Hamish and nodded his head. Without a word, Hamish got up and jogged straight up the beach to the place where the grassy banks dipped down in the middle. He ran up onto the cliffs and along towards the bothy, coming to a stop just above it. I noticed the light flickering faintly in the windows from the candles.

Duncan told us to stay where we were, then he walked off towards the rocks at the other end of the beach. When he stopped and turned round, Hamish signalled to him with what looked like a thumbs-up—it was hard to tell from there—and Duncan signalled back.

'We are celebrating the Teacher!' Duncan yelled, bending down and stepping back, as a fountain of golden sparks whooshed up into the air. He had fireworks!

'We are celebrating the Joker!'

He lit another one. This time it was crackling white like a big sparkler, with balls of red and blue shooting out.

'We are celebrating the Page!'

Milo jumped up as his firework went off with a soft shower of yellow, then green, then red.

Hamish ran down off the cliff to meet Duncan, and they both came back, beaming, to where we were sitting.

'Where did you get the fireworks?' I said.

'From the hotel. We've always got some in the stock cupboard.'

'And your parents let you?' said Tressa.

'I didn't ask them.'

Which explained why Hamish was up on the cliff, keeping a look-out.

Duncan nodded to Elspeth and she went back to the bothy, reappearing a few moments later with a plate of food. There was an apple and a chocolate bar, each cut into six pieces around a pile of crisps.

'Another time, we will have a feast,' Duncan said. 'This is just a token.'

'It's perfect,' said Tressa. 'It's like a. . .a sacrament.' You could tell she wasn't exactly sure that was the right word.

'What does that mean?' asked Duncan.

'It's when you're not eating because you're hungry, but as part of a ceremony. . .I think.' Duncan looked well impressed.

We had to go back into the bothy for the last part of the celebration. The big candle was still burning brightly on the makeshift table, and a few of the little ones were still alight along the foot of the fireplace wall. He led us to the other end of the room, where we could just make out, in the shadows, the silver foil of six new tea-lights lined up on the floor.

Duncan lit the first one, and gave the matches to Hamish. Hamish lit the second one. Elspeth lit the third one, and passed the matches on to Tressa. We weren't exactly used to striking matches when Mum, Matt or Dad weren't around, or even when they were around, come to that.

When I'm a bit nervous, I always seem to think of a joke.

'Why did the elephant eat the candle? Because he wanted a light snack!'

Tressa lit her tea-light, no bother. I broke four matches, but eventually I got mine to light too. I looked at Duncan. Milo couldn't light his own. . .could he?

Duncan took the matches. He showed Milo how to light one, blew it out, and handed him the box. The first few times Milo tried, he wasn't pressing hard enough and nothing happened. So he pressed harder, and the next few matches broke. When he finally managed to get one to light, he lost his nerve and dropped it on the dirt floor.

He looked at Duncan. 'Keep trying,' Duncan said. 'You can do it.'

I didn't actually think he could, and my attention was starting to wander. By the light of the five we had already lit, I could see lots of objects stuck between the stones in the wall. An orange rubber glove, a little cork float shaped like a doughnut, a scrap of fishing net with a dead crab hooked on by its claw.

All sorts of pebbles and shells were in that wall, and pieces of coloured glass ground smooth by the waves. On a low ridge, the row of tiny skeletons we'd noticed on the first day looked ghostly pale, the light picking out their beaks like shiny beads.

Milo finally got a match to light, and managed not to drop it. Elspeth guided his hand down to the tealight, and when it lit he literally jumped for joy. Boing, boing, look what I did!

'Before, there were only three of us,' Duncan said. 'Now there are six. Now we can close the circle.'

We joined hands around the big candle on the makeshift table and did the rhyme. *Round and round. . .can't be unbound. . .the Binding.*

Part Two: Darkness in the sky

Chapter 1

The Day Star

I definitely did not like the idea of Duncan telling us how we should behave at home. On the other hand, I definitely did like the effect it had on Tressa. If Matt forgot that he was likely to get his head chewed off and accidentally asked her to do something such as, for example, taking her muddy shoes off or passing the jam, she did it. No *you're-not-my-dad* or anything. Then, while Matt and Mum were exchanging astonished glances, she would shoot me and Milo a secret smile.

I liked the effect it had on Milo too. No more massive arguments when Mum said it was bedtime;

no more mega-tantrums when he couldn't have thirds of cake or lost a car under the dresser. Just those astonished glances and secret smiles.

I didn't think Duncan's rules would make any difference to how I behaved—I mean, I wasn't stroppy to Mum and I actually liked having Matt around—but then there was the rule about not arguing. It's amazing how much you can argue with someone and not notice. As soon as I started noticing, I discovered how fed up I was with Milo half the time. He could be such a baby, and so annoying.

'We can get that car out with a stick,' I said. 'I'll help you.'

Astonished glances, secret smiles.

Matt and Mum thought it was the simple island life and all that lovely fresh air which was making us less argumentative. It was the one thing Mum actually liked about being on Morna. She said yes, it was beautiful, and yes, it was relaxing and all that, when Matt was being a one-man Morna fan-club, but you could tell she was just saying it. She liked Matt, but she no way liked the island, and it didn't get any better when the sunshine disappeared.

After a week of bright but chilly weather, a lid of cloud closed over the island, cutting off the tops of the hills. Mum didn't want to go out for walks any more so she stayed at home with her Kindle. Matt was getting into photography, which meant he didn't care about the weather. He went out with his camera in the daytime and played about with his pictures on the laptop in the evenings.

Me, Tressa and Milo had a sort of project too. Duncan and the others were showing us 'the secret places of Morna'. The cloud stayed on the hills for days, so there wasn't any point going inland because we wouldn't see anything anyway. So we explored the coastline, taking a different section each afternoon, all the way down the low-lying east side of the island. Duncan would stride ahead, beating down the nettles and thistles with his stick, and sometimes the flowers too, making their bright heads fly up into the air.

On the first day, they took us to the seal beach, which didn't seem to have any seals. But when we went to the water's edge and sang some songs, suddenly there they were, bobbing about in the water, coming to investigate what was making the noise.

On the second day, they took us to a little lake—they called it a lochan—on the top of a cliff, right close to the edge, where the water spilled over and splashed down onto the narrow stony beach below.

'This is the leap,' Hamish said.

'Why is it called that?'

Instead of answering, he went to the neck of the lochan where the waterfall started, and jumped across. If he had slipped on the wet grass, he would have fallen over the cliff. Duncan jumped across after him. Then Elspeth. Then Tressa did it, so I had to as well. Milo wanted to, but Duncan said his legs weren't long enough, and then we all jumped back.

Another day, they took us to the wrecking rocks, where the islanders long ago used to light fires to guide ships into harbour on stormy nights, only there wasn't a harbour, and the ships would run aground on the rocks in the dark. All the sailors and cargo would be thrown into the sea, and driven towards the next bay by the tide, where later, when the storm was past, the islanders could go and pick up wood from the broken ship for their fires, and bag what they wanted of its cargo.

'They had to pick through the dead sailors to find what they were after,' Duncan said. 'Then they left the bodies there for the crows.'

You could never tell whether he was making it all up, but who cared? If they were just stories, they were brilliant ones, and being there where they were supposed to have happened made your hair stand on end.

Like when we went to the priest's stack. It was a huge column of rock standing in the edge of the sea, capped with grass. The sheer edges were full of noisy seabirds, and the smell of their fishy poos was worse than the public toilets in Grove Road Park.

Duncan said once upon a time the only people who lived on the island were three monks, but then the Vikings came. They killed two of the monks but the third one got away. While the Vikings were stealing and wrecking in the monastery, the last monk ran down to the shore where we were standing right now and swam out to the stack. He hid in a cave on the far side where no-one could see him, but there wasn't any food and years later, all they found was his bones.

Everywhere we went, Duncan had a blood-curdling story to tell, and in just the same way as stories seemed to be everywhere for Duncan, jokes were for me. A cow in a field reminded me, 'What do you call a cow eating grass? A lawn-mooer!' Rabbits on the cliffs reminded me, 'How can you tell that carrots are good for your eyes? You never see a rabbit wearing glasses!'

Thistles, hedgehogs, chickens, spiders, mud, clouds. . .everything reminded me of jokes. A lone tree huddled in a cranny made me think of 'How do you catch a squirrel? Climb up a tree and act like a nut!'

'What's a squirrel?' Elspeth said.

Me and Tressa laughed. Hamish and Duncan didn't. It looked like they didn't know what a squirrel was either. Come to think of it, there weren't going to be any squirrels in Morna because there were virtually no trees.

'Seriously?' goes Tressa. 'Haven't you ever seen one in a book?'

You could see that Duncan was annoyed, and he went striding off.

The longest walk for us was the day we went to the south light. Elspeth and Hamish met us on the track near our house, then we all went to pick up Duncan at the hotel and struck out from there around the coast towards the southern tip of the island.

Considering the north light was just a small automatic light and not a proper lighthouse at all, I don't know why I thought the south one would be bigger and better, with red and white stripes all the way to the top, like lighthouses are supposed to have, and buildings at the bottom for the lighthouse keeper to live in. Which reminds me, why did the toad become a lighthouse keeper? He had his own frog-horn!

The south light was exactly the same as the north one. We saw it as we rounded a headland, a little white marker on the highest point of the cliff. We could have walked across the open moor straight to it, but Duncan insisted we had to stay on the coast and walk round the cliffs, which was much further. I didn't mind for myself and Tressa, but it was tough on Milo, what with him only having little legs and everything.

The light was barely bigger than a triangulation point. We sat on the stony ground around the concrete base, looking out at the white-topped waves breaking over a line of rocks as sharp as crocodiles' teeth that stuck up from the sea.

'That's where the *Day Star* ran aground,' Duncan said. 'Right there on those rocks.'

I remembered the news stories, and Jean next door talking about it, when she got home from her summer in Morna—this big oil tanker breaking up on rocks right underneath a lighthouse. The captain didn't see the light because he'd got drunk and fallen asleep.

'It happened in the daytime,' Hamish said. 'There was a force ten gale.'

'The wind whipped the oil up into a vapour, and then this black mist got blown across the island,' said Elspeth. 'Everyone had to stay indoors and keep their windows shut so they didn't breathe it in.'

'But most of it stuck to the rocks and beaches like thick black treacle,' Duncan said.

'It swallowed up the seabirds and seals,' said Elspeth. 'It was terrible.'

Duncan said the worst thing was the invasion of incomers that came afterwards, when the mist had gone and the whole shoreline was dead under the slick.

'They came with their detergents, trying to save birds that were going to die anyway, breaking up the slick on the water by spraying chemicals and trying to clean it off the rocks, but they were just adding poison to the poison.'

The incomers couldn't make the shoreline clean again, and half the oil was still there when they left. But after they'd gone, nature started its work. More gales came and broke up the slick; they churned up the waves and scoured the beaches clean.

'Incomers don't understand anything,' said Duncan. 'They think they have the power, but nature is stronger. Incomers have no power here.'

Chapter 2

Good secrets, bad secrets

The noise of rain drumming on the windows woke me up. It was like a gigantic power shower, pointing straight at the front of the house. Mum made bacon sandwiches for breakfast to try and cheer us up, although the only person who really needed cheering up was her.

'When it's raining, there's absolutely nothing to do here,' she said, shaking her head. 'If it doesn't stop, I'm afraid we might just have to pack up and go home early.' She did her best to look sad.

'I think it's easing up,' said Matt, peering out at the rain. 'It'll just be a passing shower.'

'Oh, good,' goes Mum, looking like she'd found a penny and lost a pound.

Matt put the ketchup on the table and went to stand behind Mum at the cooker, sliding his arms around her waist. Tressa didn't even say one little 'yuck!' She didn't make a face or stick her fingers down her throat either. She was sooo sticking to the rules!

'When it stops,' Matt said, 'let's go to the hotel for lunch.'

'That would cost an arm and a leg,' said Mum.

'My treat,' goes Matt.

But lunchtime came and the rain still hadn't stopped. We'd played all our board games and hangman and one-word-at-a-time-stories and everything else we could think of, and still it was pouring down. Mum plonked some bread and cheese on the table for lunch. Presumably, she thought we were past cheering up by then.

We were just finishing off the last of the bread when Matt said, 'Shh! What can you hear?'

We all fell silent, listening.

'Nothing,' whispered Milo.

'Exactly,' said Matt. 'It's stopped raining! We'll be able to go down to the hotel for afternoon tea.'

Afternoon tea means cakes, which is always good, but that wasn't the only reason me and Tressa were dead keen to go to the hotel. We might meet Duncan's mum and dad, and they might be as weird as him, and what would it be like inside? Would there be candles everywhere? What if he was there? Would he pretend not to know us? Would we have to pretend not to know him as well?

We could do that. Tressa was proving to have world-class acting skills, I was nearly in her league, and even Milo was doing a fair job of pretending not to be a great big baby full of strops and tantrums.

Just walking through the gate into the hotel's walled garden felt like entering a magic land. Outside, everything was wild and windswept, grass and rocks and bogs, but inside, there were flowerbeds and bright green lawns. There was a pond with a fountain, and a patio with white-painted metal chairs; a climbing rose against one wall and actual palm trees in pots on either side of the front door.

Matt rang the bell in the lobby and a big stocky man with close-cropped dark ginger hair came out. He absolutely had to be Duncan's dad.

'Come in, come in! Welcome!' he boomed, shaking Matt's hand so hard it looked as if he was trying to pull it off. 'Edward Fairfax, at your service! Come on through!'

Mum grabbed Milo's hand and put her other one on my shoulder, so Mr Fairfax couldn't shake her hand too. What a chicken! But she didn't get off scot-free because as soon as we got into the dining room and she dropped her hand from my shoulder, Mrs Fairfax strode in through another door and grabbed it. Shake, shake, shake! 'Come in, come in, come in!' She was nearly as big as her husband, and talked just as loud.

The dining room was posh and old-fashioned, with white tablecloths and faded pictures in gold frames on the walls. It had a high ceiling with a chandelier in the middle and fancy mouldings of leaves and flowers all round the edge.

Mrs Fairfax sat us at a table near the window, looking out over the fountain, and went to get our tea. Mr Fairfax stayed to chat with Mum and Matt, looming over them as straight-backed as a soldier on parade.

'And how are you enjoying life on our little island?' he asked. Matt said it was wonderful. Such fantastic scenery! Such amazing wildlife! And so lovely for the children to have so much freedom.

Mr Fairfax beamed. But since Mum hadn't said anything, he turned to her and said sympathetically, 'Harder for the ladies, I think. They do need a bit more company. Gossip and news and suchlike.' You could tell Mum wasn't warming to him.

'It is a bit lonely sometimes,' Mrs Fairfax agreed, catching what he was saying as she brought in the tray. 'But we've got a big party coming in tomorrow. You must pop down and say hello.'

She put the silver teapots on the table in front of Mum and cleared some space for a plate of sandwich triangles with the crusts cut off. Then she disappeared again, coming back straight away with a cake-stand three layers high. On the bottom layer there were slices of fruit cake and cherry cake and Madeira. On the middle layer, there were little cupcakes with bright coloured icing and silver balls, and on the top layer there were squares of fudge and shortcake and chocolate brownies.

'Now we'll leave you to enjoy your tea,' she said. 'Just ring the bell if you need anything.'

The sandwiches and cakes were the best ever, but as we worked our way through them I couldn't help feeling just a bit disappointed that we hadn't seen Duncan. Then Mum rang the bell for some more hot water, and Duncan walked in.

'Hello, hello,' he said, sounding just like his dad. 'My mother and father said you were here—"the family from Jean's house," they said.' He grinned at Tressa, Milo and me.

'Duncan Fairfax,' he announced, offering Matt his hand. He shook Mum's hand too, as if he was a grown-up, and it was his hotel. 'My friends and I have been showing Tressa, Jack and Milo round, and they've been teaching us French cricket and that kind of thing.' He made it sound so normal. 'When Tressa, Jack and Milo have finished their tea, would it be all right for them to come out and play in the garden?' Duncan asked Mum. 'We've got croquet.'

Tressa jumped up. 'We've finished now!' she said.

The three of us followed Duncan down a long hallway and out the back door. Milo wanted to know what croquet was.

'That doesn't matter,' said Duncan. 'I just wanted to get you on your own for a minute to tell you about tomorrow. We're going swimming in the sea pool!'

'What, in this weather?' goes Tressa.

It wasn't raining any more but the air was cold and everything felt wet, from the squishy grass to the raindrops wobbling on all the flowers and leaves.

'Rain or shine,' said Duncan. 'Come after lunch, and wear your swimsuits under your clothes. You won't need towels.'

'But. . .'

'If you bring a towel, your mum will know you're going swimming, and she might say you can't. Am I wrong?'

'No, but. . .'

Duncan's dad suddenly burst out of the back door and came striding across the grass. 'Mother tells me you're going to play croquet!' he boomed. 'I'll help you set it up.'

I didn't know what croquet was but I can tell you now, it's about as exciting as standing at a bus stop. You walk around knocking balls through metal hoops, and then wait forever while everyone else has their turn. It might be all right on a scorching hot day when you just want to lie around, but on a chilly day it's torture by slowly freezing.

By the time Mum rescued us, Milo's lips were turning blue.

'It looks like there might be another downpour on the way,' she said, pointing up at the sky. 'I think we'd better be getting back.'

We walked along the top of the jetty beach together, then me and Tressa went on ahead.

'Mum's not going to let us go "rain or shine,"' I said.

'We've got to,' said Tressa. 'That's the law.'

'It might be the law that we have to go if Duncan calls a meeting, but this sounds more like just going for a swim.'

'It's at the bothy beach,' she said. 'It's bound to be a meeting.'

'Then how are we going to talk Mum round if it's pouring with rain tomorrow?'

'I don't know.' She shrugged.

That evening, the rain came in again. It rattled at the windows and drummed on the roof. Matt was at the kitchen table editing his latest batch of photos on his laptop. Milo was in bed, having miraculously gone up without a fuss.

Tressa was buried in a book and I was pretending to read, although really I was worrying about how we were going to get it past Mum to go out the next day, rain or shine.

Mum pulled her earphones out. She said it was hard to get excited about listening to the news when it felt like we were living on a different planet.

'That boy seems nice. I'm glad you've made some friends.'

I said Duncan was really clever and interesting, and he knew lots of great stories about Morna. She said it was just a shame the weather seemed to have turned, because we wouldn't be able to go outside and play if it didn't pick up. 'Still, you could always invite your friends over here.'

'It. . .it won't matter if it's raining, actually.'

I glanced across at Tressa, but she was absorbed in her book.

'We don't just play outside. We've got a den.'

Did Tressa blink? She didn't look up, so perhaps I just imagined it.

'What kind of den?' Mum was suddenly interested. 'Where is it?'

I lowered my voice.

'That's a secret, only the point is, it doesn't matter if it rains because we can play inside the den.'

Mum put her head on one side.

'So what do you do in this secret den?'

It suddenly occurred to me that she might laugh if I told her, and I was starting to wish I hadn't said anything at all. Mum saw me frown, and smiled.

'Sorry, Jack,' she said. 'I shouldn't be asking you all these questions. After all, a secret is a secret. Do you fancy a game of cards?'

We didn't ask Tressa if she wanted to join in because she thinks cards are so boring it's an insult to her intelligence to even suggest she might want to play. Anyway, she was stuck so deep into her book, she probably wouldn't have noticed if Justin I'm-so-cool from across the road, who she adores, was to magically appear beside her and give her a big sloppy kiss.

On our third round of rummy, Mum went back to the subject of secrets. There were good secrets and bad secrets, she said. 'If keeping a secret gives you a delicious feeling of excitement, it's a good secret. But if it makes you feel anxious and shifty, it's a bad one. This secret den. . .'

'Is really great,' I said.

'That's all right then,' said Mum.

It was weird, but just talking about the bothy— even though I called it a den and didn't say where it was or tell her about the candles and the fire, which she would have freaked out about—kind of made it feel less special.

The Binding was a big secret made up of so many little secrets, like the rituals and ceremonies and celebrations, and the secret of why we weren't arguing at all any more at home. I was sorry I had said anything, and I decided I definitely for certain sure would not say a single word about it to anyone again.

Matt came through from the kitchen with his laptop under his arm.

'Can I play?' he asked. 'And what about you, Tressa?'

Oh my God—he touched her shoulder! He stopped her reading! He asked her if she wanted to play cards! He had wandered into a minefield and was dancing among the mines.

Tressa looked up and smiled. She closed her book and laid it down on the arm of her chair. 'That sounds like fun.'

Mum blinked in disbelief. When she had pulled herself together enough to start dealing the cards, me and Tressa exchanged a secret smile. She was so good!

Following the rules of how to behave at home made everything feel like a game of pretend and, in a weird way, feeling fake at home made the Binding seem even more real.

Chapter 3

Swimming

Mum was cross with Milo when she found out he had spent the whole morning playing out in the wrecked van without his coat on.

'It's not that cold, actually,' Matt said, dumping his camera on the shelf by the back door and kicking off his boots. 'It's just a bit cloudy.'

'A bit cloudy as in Einstein's a bit clever,' said Mum.

Not being that cold sounded like good news to anyone who was wearing their swimsuit under their clothes.

'It's going to rain,' said Mum.

I knew she would ask how far it was to the den and I didn't want her to mention it in front of Tressa and Milo, so when they went to look at Matt's latest batch of pictures, I stayed to help with laying the table.

'It won't matter if it rains this afternoon,' I told her. 'Our den's really close by.'

'Well, just make sure Milo wears his coat,' she said. 'You should probably all take your hats and gloves as well.'

I was going to protest that we wouldn't need them and it would be a pain having to carry them around when I suddenly realised this could work our way.

'Do you think Matt would lend us his day-sack to carry them in?'

'Of course! Help yourself—it's beside the dresser.'

Tressa and me had thought of something we'd need to take to the pool with us that was too big to smuggle out in our pockets. The fact was, Milo couldn't swim. I wasn't sure he should come with us at all, but he would no way keep to the rules about how to behave at home if we told him he couldn't, and anyway Tressa reckoned he'd be all right so long as he had his armbands on. He had brought them on holiday, but one of them wouldn't deflate properly, so we couldn't get it flat.

It was nearly as big as the ball I was planning to take. You have to have the right sort of ball for swimming-pool games—not a tennis ball which will get heavy and soggy, or a small hard bouncy ball that will hurt if it hits your bare skin. The perfect swimming-pool ball is a mini-football of the kind it just so happened I'd been playing with out in the yard.

I put the ball and armbands in Matt's day-sack under the hats and gloves and then had the idea of putting my trick dog poo in as well. Swimming was just too good an opportunity to miss. They were going to love it!

After lunch, we made our getaway before Mum had a chance to change her mind. It was spitting a bit by then, but like Matt said, it wasn't cold, probably because there wasn't any wind.

We saw a smudge of smoke in the sky above the bothy. They were all inside, but the door was open, so we went straight in. A driftwood fire was crackling in the hearth, with the fish-box chairs arranged in a semi-circle in front of it. On the makeshift table there was a pile of white towels that looked orangey in the firelight, and a big silver flask.

'Hot chocolate,' Duncan said, 'for when we come out.'

He told us he always brought the towels when they were going swimming, because it was easy for him. There were gazillions of towels at the hotel and all he had to do was nick a few from the linen cupboard on the way out and dump them in the laundry baskets when he got home again.

'My parents never notice anything,' he said. 'They're always busy, specially on days like this when they've got guests coming in on the boat.'

I said we'd smuggled a few things out as well, such as for example, Milo's armbands.

'If he can't swim he can't come in the pool,' said Duncan. 'That's the rule.'

Milo's bottom lip, which had been remarkably firm for days, began to wobble. His thumb hovered, half-way to his mouth.

'But this is a good thing because I need somebody to look after my stick while we're in the pool,' said Duncan.

Milo couldn't believe the honour that was being bestowed upon him. He took the stick in both his hands with a massive grin. It was like a magic wand, magically making him happy.

'You can use it to poke around for precious objects among the seaweed that we can add to the end wall,' suggested Duncan.

Milo couldn't wait, so he bounded off to start foraging while the rest of us stripped to our swimsuits and raced down the beach to the pool. I had the ball, and no-one noticed the fake dog poo in my other hand.

We stood shivering in a line along the concrete barrier at the seaward end. It was still spitting, and the raindrops made faint circles on the surface of the water. I put the ball down on the edge of the concrete, with the dog poo hidden behind it.

Duncan suddenly plunged in, making a massive splash. Hamish went next, then Tressa, gasping and spluttering at the sudden cold.

'I told you,' Duncan said. 'Are you all right?'

Tressa's jaw seemed to be frozen shut, so she just nodded and tried to look as if she wasn't struggling to breathe. Elspeth jumped in, which meant I was the only one left and there wasn't any getting out of it.

You know when you've been outside on a frosty day without your hat and scarf and your ears hurt and your chin's gone numb and your fingers feel like they're going to fall off? And then, if it goes on, the cold creeps into your bones so you can't even get warm again when you've been back indoors in front of the fire for hours?

Well, it was like that, only instant.

Duncan, Hamish and Elspeth were thrashing up and down the pool to warm up, and me and Tressa knew we had to do the same, but we just couldn't. As well as the fact it was too cold to breathe, my skeleton felt like someone had sprayed it with dry ice so it had gone all hard and brittle.

Duncan and Hamish were laughing.

'C-c-c-come on,' Tressa said, pushing off from the side.

I grabbed the ball and threw it into the middle of the pool. Hamish dived for it but it bounced away from him on the wave of water he had made, giving me a chance to go for it myself. Chasing a ball is the best way I know to forget about bad stuff, such as the fact that you're colder than an ice cube in a slushie.

I knew they wouldn't notice the dog poo straight away. It's an old magician's trick—distract them with something interesting to look at, such as a mini-football flying through the air, and they won't see anything else.

So it was only after we'd been chasing the ball for a while that Elspeth, swimming to the edge for a rest, put her hand on the concrete and let out a scream.

'Yuk! That's disgusting! I nearly put my hand in it!'

We all swam over to see what she had found.

'But how did it get there?' said Hamish. 'Who's got a dog that comes down to this beach?'

'Nobody comes down to this beach at all,' said Duncan.

'Somebody must,' said Elspeth. 'And if their dog's doing its business near the pool then the tide could be washing it in.'

Tressa squealed. 'There might be dog poo in the pool!'

She started clambering out, and everyone else did too. We stood on the concrete, bending down to examine the fake dog poo. It looked exactly like the real thing.

'We're going to have to clear it up and bury it,' said Duncan.

'I'll do that,' I said. 'I don't mind!'

I picked it up in my hand and they all gave a yell of disgust.

'Got you!' I said, holding it out to them so they could see it was fake. I tossed it into the pool, where it bobbed on the surface, nudging up to the ball. They all burst out laughing, even Tressa, and I plunged back in again before they had a chance to push me.

They didn't know how to play under-the-legs or f-i-s-h-y or water-ball-he, so I had a great time teaching them, and Duncan said it was the best fun they had ever had in the pool. I was everyone's favourite person, except Tressa's. You could see she was fed up that I was getting all the attention, and you couldn't really blame her. I mean, which would you rather be, the Joker or the Teacher?

The sky went suddenly dark. There was a downpour on the way, but no-one wanted to get out of the pool because we were having such a laugh. I thought we might have time for one more game.

'Who wants to play dog-poo pig-in-the-middle?'

Before we could start, the skies opened and the rain came pouring down, huge drops hammering onto the rocks and bouncing off the surface of the pool. We saw Milo go haring across the beach towards the bothy. I realised that technically, since we were already soaked and suitably dressed, that didn't mean we necessarily had to go indoors.

We all looked at Duncan for a decision, but before he had a chance to say anything, Tressa announced, 'I am the eyes and ears of the Lawmaker and I wish to make a report!'

We blinked at her through the rain. Then Hamish said, 'You can't do that here. We'll have to go in.'

We climbed out of the pool and ran up the beach, with the rain beating down on us. Then we dived into the bothy and all grabbed a towel. Duncan said Tressa's report would have to wait because we had to get dry first, warm ourselves by the fire and have our hot chocolate.

Was he a bit annoyed with Tressa for forcing him to go all serious and put on the Judgement when we were all having fun? Or was it just me? Because I *was* annoyed—I was properly annoyed.

We towelled ourselves dry and got dressed in front of the fire. Duncan had brought a comb so we wouldn't have tell-tale swimming-hair when we got home. Hamish lit the candles around the fireplace and along the ledge above.

Duncan took some plastic beakers out of his pack and shared out the hot chocolate. He'd also brought some soft bread rolls for us to dunk in it. He had thought of everything and it should have been perfect, but Tressa's report was hanging over us like the thirteenth fairy nobody had wanted to invite.

We tried to ignore it and get the mood back by talking about our swim. What was the best bit? What was the funniest bit? Was it like me and Tressa had expected it to be? The flickering firelight lit up our faces and made our skin tingle with warmth. We were all laughing, but we were also waiting, and eventually Duncan said we had better make the circle.

He moved the makeshift table to the middle of the room, and we dragged our fish-box seats into position around it. It felt cold, away from the fire, and darker too until Elspeth brought out the big candle and Hamish lit it.

'Teacher, you have a report to make,' Duncan said to Tressa, in a tone that clearly said, *this had better be good.*

Tressa stood up.

'My brother, the Joker, has told our mother about the bothy.'

They all gave a gasp of surprise.

Elspeth passed Hamish the Judgement, Hamish passed it to Duncan and Duncan unfolded it and placed it on his head. He hadn't worn it since Milo had told on me for asking Mum about the berries.

Duncan stood up, and motioned to the rest of us to stand as well.

'Is this true?' he asked.

I nodded. 'But I didn't say it was a bothy—I said it was a den—and I never mentioned where it was. I said it was secret.'

'That's all very well but now they know we have a den, they might come looking for it,' Duncan said.

I hadn't thought of that, but what was I supposed to have done?

'If I hadn't told Mum we had a den, she would one hundred per cent not have let us come out "rain or shine". Tressa knows that, but she didn't have any better ideas.'

The rain hammering on the roof slates seemed to back up my argument, but Duncan still took a step back. One by one, they all did the same, until I was left on my own in the middle.

'You are guilty of breaking the most sacred law of the Binding,' said Duncan. 'Your punishment is this. Tomorrow afternoon, we will meet at the hotel and walk out to the south light, but while the rest of us follow the coast you will go directly across the field.'

And that's it? I have to cross a field? Hamish grinned at Duncan. I smiled at Elspeth, but she wouldn't meet my eye.

Duncan said, 'Now we reward the eyes and ears with gold.'

Elspeth brought the pencil tin out of the box and handed it to him. He took out two chocolate bars, which he gave to Tressa. I wished I could wipe that smug look off her face.

'One more thing,' he said. 'Until the Joker has done his punishment, he is outside the circle, and that means you must not talk to him except when you have to because there are people around.'

I didn't mind about the field, but that seemed a bit mean. Maybe Duncan didn't think Tressa and Milo would actually stick to it, but I knew they would. Milo always did what Duncan told him, and Tressa couldn't talk to me or else he'd rat her in.

Milo would love to have the chance to tell on me again, I thought, seeing the way he looked at Tressa as she unwrapped her chocolate.

Chapter 4

The punishment

I wasn't going to give those couple of snitches, Tressa and Milo, the chance to ignore me all morning so I hung out with Matt. I think he was avoiding Mum because she had totally stopped making the effort to hide the fact that she was mega bored in Morna and really wanted to go home.

We went up the hill behind the house again, not to the top but just up to the cloud-line. Matt was creating a whole album called 'Clouds', which Mum said was 'making a virtue of necessity'. He also had quite a few great shots of rain.

If Jean had shown us her rainy-day photos instead of all the sunny ones, Mum would definitely never have agreed to come. But Matt said he thought the island was beautiful in all the weathers, and he could just sit there for hours enjoying the sights and sounds of nature. Considering he liked peace and quiet so much, you couldn't help feeling sorry for him, that he'd somehow wandered into a household full to overflowing with the sights and sounds of Milo, Tressa and me.

When we three eventually set off down to the hotel in the afternoon, I was expecting them to talk to each other and ignore me, but in the event they didn't talk at all. It felt a bit weird and embarrassing, but nowhere near as weird and embarrassing as when Mrs Fairfax hello-hello-helloed us in for some juice and home-made shortbread with Duncan, Hamish and Elspeth, and everyone acted normal.

The minute we left the hotel, they all stopped talking to me. Anyone seeing us go by wouldn't have noticed anything odd, just one kid in a group who didn't feel like joining in. But there wasn't anyone around to see us go by as we left the scattering of houses and struck out around the coast.

It felt much further than when we'd done it before. What was the point? If walking across a field was Duncan's idea of a punishment, couldn't he have chosen one a bit closer to our houses?

When we came in sight of the south light, we stopped. Duncan told me to walk in a straight line across to the light, touch it, and then come back along the coast to meet up with them. I shrugged a 'whatever' and started walking.

The ground was tufty and tussocky, with cushions of brown spongy moss and deep boggy bright green pools. You couldn't stride across so much as pick your way through. I didn't look back at them, but I could hear from the sound of their voices that they had set off and were walking along the coast towards the light as well.

When I was about half-way to the light there was a sudden whoosh in the sky above me, a shadow flickered across the ground in front of me, and a massive brown bird swooped down at me from behind. I felt the rush of air from its wings as I screamed in surprise and fell to my knees.

It flew low across the boggy grass, wheeled and came straight back towards me, flying at eye-level.

It had a big body, wide wings and a heavy beak. I had never seen anything like it. I got a flash of its hard mean eye before I dropped right down to the ground and threw my arms over my head.

Away to my left, I heard Duncan laughing.

'Get up!' he yelled. 'Keep going!'

I hadn't even got to my feet before the bird came at me again from behind, and then a second one swept in from the side. They circled and swooped, going for my head, flying straight towards my face.

I ducked and dipped, flailing my arms above me, but my feet seemed frozen to the spot. When one of them actually hit the side of my head with its wing, I totally panicked and ran.

I tripped and stumbled across the tufty ground, waving my arms above my head, and screams came out of my mouth all on their own, every time the huge birds swooped. Then, just as suddenly as it had started, it stopped. The birds flew away behind me and didn't come back.

I looked across at the others, and even from that distance, I could see that they were laughing. The only one who wasn't laughing was Elspeth. I could hear the rest of them as I trudged the rest of the way, to touch the cold white wall of the light.

When I met up with them on the cliffs, Tressa, Milo, Hamish and Duncan were grinning like a pack of hyenas.

'You did look funny!' said Milo.

He was too young to know better, but the rest of them were idiots.

'Don't look so cross!' goes Duncan. 'You weren't in any real danger!'

'They're just bonxies protecting their chicks,' said Hamish. 'The worst you could get is a bash on the head with their beak.'

Duncan looked puffed up and pleased with himself.

'It was a punishment fit for a Joker!' he declared with a grin.

We set off for home, all of them chatting about how funny I had looked, ducking and leaping and screaming across the open moorland like a mad thing. They actually seemed to expect me to join in, but my heart was still pounding and my stomach churning from being so scared. I would have thrown up, only I didn't want to give them something else to laugh at.

We reached the first farm, with Duncan slightly ahead, happily beating down the thistles and nettles with his stick.

'Tell us a joke!' he said, looking back over his shoulder at me. 'You're the one with the great sense of humour!' It sounded friendly, but it felt like a taunt.

Everywhere I looked, there were jokes. A cow in the field reminded me—what do you get if you sit under a cow? A pat on the head! A sheep rubbing her side on fence post reminded me—what do you get if you cross a sheep with a kangaroo? Little woolly jumpers! The sound of a bee in the farmer's garden made me think, why do bees hum? Because they've forgotten the words!

Jokes were everywhere, but I wasn't in the mood, and I said I couldn't think of a single one. It was too soon. I would get over it, obviously, but I wasn't ready to yet.

When we got to the hotel, Duncan said, 'Everyone meet at the bothy after tea tonight, all right?' Then he went inside and the rest of us carried on along the top of the jetty beach. Milo and Hamish walked ahead with Tressa, and Elspeth hung back with me.

Neither of us said anything, and I wished she would go away and leave me alone. I remembered the way she couldn't meet my eye in the bothy, when Duncan had handed out the punishment. She knew what was going to happen. She knew why it had to be that field.

Back at the house, I played footie against the wall while Mum and Matt were making the tea. Gradually, the churning inside me stopped, soothed by the steady thud-bounce-kick, thud-bounce kick, thud-bounce-kick.

Then thoughts came in, the way they always do when you play ball against a wall on your own. I suddenly thought about Benjie and the zip-wire we made in his garden, and the ground-sheet water slide, and football at the park.

I didn't feel like going to the bothy after tea. I wanted to tell Tressa and Milo to go without me, this one time, but when I imagined myself doing that, I knew Tressa would laugh and tell me to get over it, and Milo would say, 'We have to go when the Lawmaker decides—that's the law!'

So we told Mum and Matt we were going out to play, and Mum said, in that case, she and Matt might go down to the hotel and meet the visitors.

'We'll only be gone an hour,' said Matt. 'We'll be back before you get home.'

Chapter 5

In the manner of the word

The firelight flickered across the stone walls, and the waves rumbled on the shore outside. They had set the bothy out in a new way, with the makeshift table at one end, away from the fire, and the fish-box seats pushed back against the walls to make a big space in the middle.

There was a cluster of tea-lights on the floor in each corner, their bright little flames floating in puddles of light. Duncan produced a cardboard box and when he opened the flaps, we could see it was full of individually-wrapped biscuits, which gleamed like jewels in the candlelight.

'These are the prizes,' he said. 'We're going to have a games night!'

'Wow!' said Milo, feasting his eyes. 'Your parents are really nice to give us all those!'

'It's no big deal,' said Duncan. 'We've got loads of them at the hotel.'

He was acting as if nothing important had happened. I had broken the rules, but I had paid the price, end of story. As far as he was concerned, everything could go back to normal.

Maybe he had chosen a games night because he wanted everything to go back to precisely how it had been in the moments before the telling and the punishment, when we were all larking around in the pool.

Maybe Tressa's telling and my punishment were things he didn't want, but had to play along with, because he was the Lawmaker, and that was his role. The punishment was horrible, but then what would be the point in a punishment that didn't hurt?

Duncan was the Lawmaker and he had played his part, now it was up to me to organise some games, because that was the part I had to play. Seeing as everyone else was behaving as if nothing important had happened, I could too, even though I was still feeling angry inside.

First we played animal-vegetable-mineral, which they already knew, and then charades, which they didn't. We'd only learnt it ourselves at Christmas, staying with Auntie Cath, but we'd gone on playing it for weeks after we got home. Then Matt moved in and Mum had to stop playing and turn referee, sorting out all the aggro between him and Tressa.

In case you've never played it, charades is an acting game. You take turns miming the title of a film or book or TV show and your team has to try and guess what it is. Duncan, Elspeth and Hamish took to it like ducks to water, but that was no surprise—they were acting all the time.

So I suggested another acting game, 'in the manner of the word'. What happens is, one person goes outside while all the others agree a word ending in '-ly', such as 'gloomily' or 'dramatically'.

When they've chosen the word, they call the person back in and he or she asks them to do things 'in the manner of the word'. They might say, 'Elspeth, make a sandwich in the manner of the word,' and then she has to pretend she's making a sandwich gloomily or dramatically or whatever.

The guesser can have as many guesses as they like, and tell everyone to do as many things as they like— 'Tressa, clean your teeth in the manner of the word', 'Hamish, dance in the manner of the word', 'Milo, put your shoes on in the manner of the word.' The game goes on until they either guess the word or have to give up and ask what it was.

We played for ages and I thought they'd totally got it, but then it was Tressa's turn to go outside and instead of us all making suggestions and choosing the word together, Duncan said, 'This time, the word is "normally".'

'But. . .that won't work,' I told him. 'If we're acting normally, she won't be able to guess it. It's got to be something specific, like "angrily". How about "angrily"?'

'I think "normally" will work,' Duncan said.

You couldn't help feeling sorry for Tressa. She got us putting our coat on in the manner of the word, and drinking a glass of juice, and reading a book, and walking round the room, and, and, and. . . She kept going and guessing for ages, until she couldn't think of a single other thing to ask us.

'This is impossible!' she said, after a squillion years of guessing. 'You're not doing anything out of the ordinary. You're all just acting normally.'

'Yes!' goes Duncan, punching the air. We fell about laughing.

'What?' Tressa looked confused.

'That's the word,' said Hamish. 'Normally!'

Tressa grinned at us. 'You rotters!'

'It was Duncan's idea,' said Milo. 'Jack said you'd never guess it, but Duncan said you would, and you did!'

Duncan gave Tressa her prize, then turned the box upside-down to show there weren't any more left. He crushed the box under his foot and put it on the fire.

'Let's make the circle now,' he said, getting up to move the table into the middle of the room.

We dragged our fish-box seats into their normal places around it. Elspeth placed the box on the table. She took out the cloth of Judgement and the candle-holder and the big candle, and Hamish lit it. Her fingers were as delicate as butterflies as she brought out the papers and the silver pen, and put them on the table in front of her.

This dance they did seemed to move us into a different place, from the games night to the Binding, in a few well-practiced moves.

Duncan said, 'I suggested "normally" because that's how you will have to act when you're getting the food for the Feast of the Ancestors, which is tomorrow.' He looked at me. 'Like all the business of the Binding, this is secret.' His blue eyes gleamed in the candlelight.

'Because it's secret,' he said, 'we can't buy the food and we can't ask for it. We have to take it without telling anyone.'

'But, isn't that stealing?' said Tressa.

We all looked at Duncan. He looked steadily back.

'How do you think Elspeth and Hamish got the food for the celebration on the beach?' he said. 'How do you think I got these prizes for tonight? If you act normally, and don't take anything that'll be missed, you'll easily get away with it.'

He stood up, and then we all stood up.

'We have to do what the Lawmaker decides,' Hamish reminded everyone.

'Don't eat much tea, and bring as much food as you can,' said Duncan. 'Let's make this feast the best one we've ever had!'

We joined hands and the circle turned.

In the winding, round and round
What we wind can't be unwound
What we bind can't be unbound
The Binding

Tressa and Milo were really excited.

'I wonder why it's called the Feast of the Ancestors,' she said, as we tramped up the track towards the house.

'What is "ancestors"?' asked Milo.

I told them what Elspeth had told me, about Duncan being descended from the first King of Morna, who came from Ireland and rode through battlefields on a white charger up to its knees in blood.

'Is that true?' asked Tressa. I shrugged. She said, 'I hope he tells us the whole story at the feast!'

'I'm going to take that big lump of cheese in the fridge,' said Milo.

Tressa said if he did that, Mum was bound to notice. 'You've got to be clever. I'll help you.'

As soon as we walked in the door, we could tell Mum was fed up and Matt was trying to jolly her along.

'How was the hotel?' asked Tressa. 'Did you meet the new visitors?'

Mum said yes, they did, but they turned out to be total weirdos. All they wanted to do was go off on their own with their binoculars and cameras. If Matt noticed she was basically calling him weird, he didn't show it.

'What did you kids get up to?' he asked.

'We played some games,' said Milo.

'Yes,' said Tressa, steering him towards the kitchen. 'And we're really hungry now. OK if we get a snack?' She gestured me to go with them, but I didn't meet her eye. My stomach had started churning again, thinking about the horror of the field, and them laughing at me, and then the games night, like nothing important had happened. I was reeling like I'd just got off a rollercoaster ride.

Anyway, I wanted to stick around and talk to Mum and Matt. Going to the hotel and meeting people had seemed like the only way Mum might start enjoying Morna, and if that hadn't worked, what was going to happen now?

'I was thinking,' Mum said to Matt. 'Maybe the whole summer is a bit too long to be away? I mean, we've both got work to do at home before the beginning of term, and the children—'

'It's the chance of a lifetime,' Matt interrupted her. 'Something completely different.'

It was different all right.

'It would be a shame not to make the most of it,' he said.

If she noticed he was basically calling her a grumpy-guts who ought to stop complaining, she didn't let on.

'Jack!' Tressa called me from the doorway. 'Don't you want to get some food?'

'No, I'm all right, thanks.'

She gave me a look which clearly said, 'They're busy trying not to have a row, and that means they're not going to notice—this is your chance!'

'So you don't think we might go home a bit earlier than we planned?' said Mum, ignoring the interruption. Tressa disappeared back into the kitchen.

Matt said, 'I know what we need—a plan! Let's make a list of all the places we haven't seen on the island yet, and try to visit them. I bet Jack could help us with that.'

Chapter 6

A cake fit for a feast

'Oh, God, seriously?' said Mum, when she opened the curtains the next morning. 'More rain?'

On the upside, me, Milo and Tressa didn't have any plans for the day; on the downside, Matt did, and there was no way he was going to get Mum out of the house to go and look at stacks and standing stones in the pouring rain.

Tressa and Milo were happy because more time at home meant more time to plot secret raids on the cupboards and fridge. They had already taken lots of stuff and I hadn't got anything, so Tressa was giving me grief.

'What's wrong with you?' she said. 'We've had loads of chances. Look what me and Milo have already got, and Mum hasn't noticed a thing!'

She opened her bedside drawer to reveal half a dozen sandwich bags, neatly tied. A few handfuls of peanuts in one, a cheese sandwich cut into little triangles in another; a couple of biscuits, some currants and raisins, six squares from Matt's big box of home-made fudge.

Besides the sandwich bags, there were also the two packets of crisps she and Milo had asked for at snack-time that morning and their bananas from bedtime the night before. I'd eaten mine.

'Pull your finger out,' said Tressa. 'Me and Milo have done our bit, now you've got to do yours.'

Milo came bounding in holding up his two fists proudly. He emptied his hands on the bedspread with a rattle of dried macaroni. Tressa said that was no good, you couldn't eat it uncooked, but Milo said, 'Yes, you can—I've tried it! But you can't eat dry lentils.' He stuck his tongue out in disgust.

'Have you been trying everything in the cupboard?' Tressa was horrified. 'You'll get us caught! That's enough now, Milo. You've found lots of food and Duncan will be really pleased with you. It's Jack's turn to get some now.'

She put the macaroni in a new sandwich bag, tied the top and placed it beside the others in the drawer.

'Come on, Jack—me and Milo will distract them for you.'

Mum and Matt didn't need any distracting because they were already in the middle of something. Mum had made a decision.

'This really isn't working for me, Matt. I've decided I definitely want to go home.'

That took him by surprise. You could see he was wondering what to say. You could tell Mum was expecting him to say, 'All right then, Dee, in that case, we might as well all go.'

He didn't. Which meant Mum kind of had to push on.

'The children will have to come with me, of course. It wouldn't be fair to ask you to look after them up here on your own.'

He'd have to say it now, otherwise he'd be breaking up their very first family holiday together, plus he'd have to stay up here in the middle of nowhere with no-one to keep him company.

But he still didn't say anything.

'This is your chance!' Tressa hissed at me, trying to steer me into the kitchen. I shook my arm free.

'I'm not saying it hasn't been good,' Mum said to Matt. 'It's been. . . well. . .'

Matt found his tongue.

'But the children are having a lovely time.'

He was going to argue it!

'Come on!' Tressa said, grabbing my arm again.

I shook her off. She shrugged and disappeared into the kitchen. We could hear Milo foraging out there and she probably wanted to stop him before he taste-tested anything else, such as, for example, the raw dirty vegetables.

'The children always enjoy their summer,' Mum said to Matt, 'even when we don't go anywhere.'

I thought she was going to mention Dad. That would be a low move, to say we'd be happier at home because we could get to see him, when here we were on our first ever family holiday with Matt. Besides,

Dad was totally cool with us spending the summer holidays here; we were going to spend every weekend in September together instead.

If she mentioned Dad, what would Matt say? I couldn't guess because I didn't know him well enough yet.

'But we're here now,' Matt said. 'And everyone's happy. . .except you.'

Was he going to say she should make an effort, for the sake of the children if not for him? That would be his low move, suggesting she didn't care about her children as much as herself. Dad had tried that when she got Head of Department and, believe me, it hadn't turned out to be a good idea.

'Look, I don't want us to fall out over this,' Mum said.

I pretended I was Googling stuff on Mum's laptop and not sticky-beaking their conversation, waiting for everything to kick off. I didn't really need to pretend though—they seemed to have forgotten I was there.

That's how it felt before Dad left to live with Donna. He and Mum couldn't even talk about what to have for tea without it turning into a massive row, and when they were yelling at each other they didn't seem to notice us at all.

That was when Nee-na got superglued into Milo's fist, and Tressa started doing those deep-dives into books. I had *A thousand super-funny jokes for kids* that Uncle Max had given me for my birthday, and it wasn't like a story, where your mind could wander, but pictures you could see straight away in your head, like the flea prowling on the hairy and the elephant eating the candle and the rabbits wearing glasses.

What's more, with jokes, you didn't need the book. You could remember them, and make those pictures in your head whenever you wanted to. By the time Dad left, I knew all the thousand super-funny jokes by heart.

Matt said, 'Look, I get it, Dee. This isn't your kind of holiday. But it is mine. What say we stay here now and do whatever you'd like to do next year?'

'But we've already been here a couple of weeks, and that's enough for a holiday.'

Matt said he didn't understand why Mum was in such a hurry—they had the whole summer. 'Like you always say, it's the one good thing about teaching.'

What do you get when you cross a snowman with a vampire? That's what I was thinking. Frostbite! Why did the traffic light turn red? You would too if you had to change in the middle of the street!

'Well, I think we should be at home for at least some of the holiday because. . .'

No, Mum—don't!

'. . .because the children are missing their days out with their father.'

Matt looked stunned, as if she'd slapped him in the face.

What do you call a doctor with eight arms? A doctopus! Imagine that. An octopus in a white coat, wearing a stethoscope. He could listen to your heart at the same time as taking your pulse, feeling the glands in your neck, answering the phone, scratching his chin and writing a prescription.

'Are you sure that's what this is about?' Matt asked. 'If you think the children want to go home, let's ask them. Jack?'

I glanced up from the computer, trying to look as if I had no idea what they'd been talking about.

'I'm looking for. . .' An ad for cupcakes popped up on the screen. 'I'm looking for a recipe.'

'A recipe?'

'Yes, I want to make a cake. Can you show me how?'

'Of course,' said Mum. 'We can do it later, when Matt and I have finished talking.'

I didn't like them talking. I didn't want them to go back to talking.

'But I have to do it right now.'

'Why? What's the rush?'

I felt like I was running into trouble, same as when you're dribbling up the field, eyes on the ball, not noticing you're heading straight for a defender.

'I need it for later on.'

'You need it?'

'Yes. . .' I glimpsed Tressa in the doorway out of the corner of my eye.

'Why?' said Mum.

I had to have a reason and, come to think of it, I did have a reason. I needed to get some food and I didn't want to steal it, especially when Mum and Matt were arguing.

'We're having a feast.'

As soon as the words were out, it was like the huge birds came swooping down again. My heart raced and my stomach lurched, but it was too late to run away.

Mum got up with a sigh. She wanted to keep on talking to Matt nearly as much as I wanted her not to. I Googled 'cakes' and clicked on a recipe site, so I had a coffee sponge up on the screen when she came over. I tilted the laptop towards her.

'No need for that!' she said. 'It's very simple. Eggs, flour, sugar and marge—we've got everything we need in the cupboard.'

There were little spills of flour on the shelf around the bag. Really, Milo—flour? Mum absent-mindedly wiped them up and then went on to wipe up the sprinkles around the sugar.

These days, she said, you would use the food-mixer to make a cake, but as there wasn't one in Jean's house, it was a good thing she remembered how to do it by hand, the way her own mother had taught her.

We weighed out some sugar and marge and took turns beating them together with a wooden spoon. Mum could do it really fast, but the spoon didn't seem to work for me. I felt slow and clumsy.

We measured the flour and beat the eggs in a jug, and added them bit by bit, alternately, until the mixture was thick and creamy. Then Mum divided it between two tins and let me lick the bowl. She asked me if it was someone's birthday and that was why we were having a feast, but I said no and changed the subject.

'What can we decorate it with?'

'We'll need some icing sugar and perhaps some sweets from the shop. You could ask Matt to pop down there with you while I stay and watch the oven. He loves going out in all this drizzle and rain.'

Milo was having a snooze on the bedroom floor among his cars, probably worn out from the excitement of turning into a sneaky little thief, but Tressa wanted to come with us. I thought she was on the snoop, in case I gave her anything else to tell on me for. But as it turned out, she had a different reason for coming.

Matt bought some icing sugar and a packet of chocolate buttons, plus a tube of coloured sprinkles which we found out when we got home were four years over the date stamp. Then he stood around chatting to the shopkeeper while I had a look through the books and games on the shelves by the door.

Instead of looking through them with me, Tressa stayed beside Matt, pretending to be interested in what he was saying. It was odd. I mean, being polite and doing what you're told was one thing, but there was absolutely nothing in the rules that said you had to suck up.

I was wondering what she was up to when I saw her hand drop down from inside her coat cuff, scoop up a carrot from the sack on the floor and pull it up inside her sleeve. Matt noticed the movement, but didn't see what she'd done.

'You look a bit flushed, Tress,' he said.

She hates it when he calls her that.

'It's being out in all this lovely weather!' said the shopkeeper, smiling.

There were only a few spots of rain as we walked back up to the house, and the sky was looking brighter. Matt asked us what was the most amazing place the island children had shown us, because he was going to have to get out the big guns if he was going to persuade Mum that she wanted to stay.

'The beach with the seals,' Tressa said, without hesitation. 'We can show you on the map.'

She did that when we got home. There she was, chatting to Matt, as if all this creeping around being good and pretending had magically made her really like him.

Me and Mum decorated the cake and when we'd finished I found Tressa lurking in the hallway, waiting for a chance to get in and peel her stolen carrot, chop it up and put the pieces in a sandwich bag.

But after all our distractions, by lunchtime they were back at it again. Matt mentioned the seal beach and Mum told him that the queen of the seals herself, all dressed up in diamonds and furs, could not entice her outside in this filthy weather.

'Enough's enough,' she said. 'We're leaving.'

Matt looked at her. Then he glanced at each of us.

'OK, if that's what you want,' he said. 'But I think, if it's all right with you, I'll stay on.'

Chapter 7

Hidden things

'I'm not going home!' Milo said, through a mouthful of beans.

Tressa shot him a warning look. You could see she didn't want to go either, but we had to do what our parents told us, that was the rule. I know Duncan said Matt counted as a parent, but if they didn't agree about what we should do, surely Mum would count more?

Before the birds, I would definitely have wanted to stay, too. The bothy, the candles, the sea-pool, the beach, the Binding—it was weird and exciting and you just wanted to keep going back. But now, it didn't feel safe. At any moment, you could think you were doing the right thing and find yourself out in the cold, waiting for your punishment. You could think, 'Walking across a field—that's no punishment!' and find yourself down on your knees in the mud, with everyone laughing at you.

'Will you be all right here on your own?' Mum asked Matt.

I suddenly imagined it—all of us getting on the boat except Matt, and him waving to us from the beach. If that happened, it might be the beginning of the end for him and Mum, and although Tressa made such a fuss about it, the fact was that things had been much better since he had moved in. Whatever we decided about staying or going, the most important thing was that we all did it together.

Milo abandoned his beans and got down, which we're not normally allowed to do without asking, but Mum didn't tell him off. In fact, she got up to clear the table, so Tressa and me had to wolf down our last few mouthfuls.

'Can I leave the washing up to you two?' asked Mum.

'Of course,' said Tressa.

'Who are you, and what have you done with my daughter?' said Mum, with a smile.

After we'd done the washing up, Tressa went upstairs and I was about to follow, when I heard Mum and Matt talking in the living room. I felt bad about eavesdropping, but I told myself it wasn't really listening behind the door so much as overhearing something and not moving away.

Mum was saying, 'I shouldn't have said that about the children missing their father.'

'No, it was a fair point,' said Matt. 'I should have thought about it myself. This is all a bit new to me.'

Mum said whether it was a fair point or not, she still wished she hadn't said it. It was just that she'd thought her wanting to go home would be enough to persuade him to come too, and when it wasn't, well. . .

I couldn't catch the next bit, so I moved up really close and put my ear to the door.

'I didn't want to say anything in front of the children,' said Mum, 'but I'm feeling uncomfortable about them going off on their own all the time. I know it's irrational because what harm can they come to, but it just feels odd.'

'You're used to being more in control,' said Matt.

'I'm supposed to be—I'm their mother.'

They were talking much more quietly now, and I had to really press my ear against the wood.

'I think something's going on,' Mum said. 'I just can't put my finger on it.'

Matt said he had to bow to her greater knowledge, what with him not even being a parent, let alone our parent. He hadn't spotted anything different, except that Tressa seemed to be warming to him, which was actually another reason he quite wanted to stay.

'So, what are we going to do?' asked Mum. 'Let's either both stay here or both go home.'

I started breathing again, then stopped, in case they heard me.

'You love being here so much and you're right, the children do seem to be having a wonderful time. . .'

'Yes, but you know your children better than I do. . .'

They went even quieter, and I tried to move closer to the door, but then everything went fuzzy like it does when you hold a seashell over your ear, you just hear a whooshing of waves. I suddenly realised they'd actually stopped talking, which meant they might be on the move any minute. I backed away and slipped upstairs to my bedroom.

I know you shouldn't earwig a private conversation, but I wasn't sorry I did. It was a big relief to know that Mum and Matt wanted to stick together, either staying or leaving early, so now it was simply a case of which one was going to back down. I might not know Matt very well, but knowing Mum, I was pretty sure it wouldn't be her.

So this feast might be one of the last times we went to the Binding, and I wanted it to be nice. It was a shame, but I couldn't take the cake because there was no way I could have smuggled a whole cake out without Mum knowing; everyone would know I'd asked instead of stealing, and then things could get nasty again.

Tressa might still tell on me, of course, but Milo couldn't because he didn't even know I'd told Mum about the feast, being as how he was busy sampling all the stuff in the cupboards at the time.

So I put the cake in a Tupperware box and hid it in one of the sheds, in the grass-box of an old lawn-mower. Later, when Tressa gave me her and Milo's stash to put in Matt's day-sack, neither of us mentioned it.

We found Duncan and the others sitting on the grass outside the bothy. It wasn't raining, and there were little patches of clear sky between the shifting clouds. They had laid all the food out on an old cupboard door that had been washed up on the beach a few days before.

As well as the food, there were six cans of cola that Duncan had brought from the hotel bar and two empty plates, waiting for our offerings. I handed the sandwich bags to Tressa and Milo, and they arranged the food on the plates. Then she looked at me expectantly.

'What?' I said.

She frowned, but she didn't say anything. We went down onto the sand and helped Duncan, Hamish and Elspeth to make a ring of big stones. Then we gathered armfuls of driftwood from the pile behind the bothy and stacked it up nearby.

Duncan gave Milo his stick and told him he was in charge of keeping the seagulls away from the food while the rest of us were building the fire. Hamish put a match to half a dozen sticks inside the ring of stones, and we sat round waiting for it to catch. As the fire grew from a few pale flames to a warm red glow, we took turns adding larger pieces of wood.

When the fire was burning strongly, we carried the old door with all the food on it down onto the sand, and we had the feast, and still Tressa didn't say anything. Milo told the others proudly about all the things he'd found, and his adventures in taste-testing. He said Tressa had made the cheese sandwich, and they'd both saved their crisps and bananas instead of eating them.

'What about Jack?' Duncan asked. Then, turning to me, 'What did you bring?'

Tressa straight away cut in.

'Jack got the carrot. He took it from right under their noses in the shop this morning. He stuffed it up his sleeve!'

'I didn't know that,' Milo said.

'You were asleep on your car mat,' said Tressa.

You'd have thought Duncan would be impressed by my apparent shoplifting, but he just looked at me steadily. I tried to look straight back, but his eyes were like blue searchlights that could see right inside your brain.

When all the food was gone, we gathered more closely around the fire, and Duncan told us stories about Morna from across the mists of time. He told us about the monks who came from the mainland, putting out to sea in an open boat with no oars, trusting God to bring them safely to land. Wherever they landed, he said, they believed that was where God wanted them to be.

He told us about the Vikings who came with their three great leaders, Haakon the Hairy, Olaf the Unyielding and One-eyed Erik. He described them so well that we could almost see them, coming up the beach with their horned helmets and shields gleaming in the fading light.

He told us about his own ancestor who came over the sea from Ireland to rule as the first king of Morna. He built his castle on the site where the hotel was now, and although the castle was long gone, there was still a dungeon underneath the ground that you could get to through a secret passage.

Duncan said that one of his ancestors was a seer, which meant he could tell the future, and he could also look right into a person's soul and see all the things they tried to keep hidden. Such abilities, he said, could be passed down.

The fire burned red and the beach grew darker, and the moon appeared in a patch of sky where the clouds had opened up. I hadn't even realised it was there.

All of us had tried to hide things from Mum and thought we were getting away with it, but it turned out she knew something was going on. Now Tressa and me were trying to hide something from Duncan, and he knew too.

I thought about my cake, hidden in the shed. I wondered if rats had found it and eaten through the plastic box, or maybe ants could have come and crawled under the lid. That was the problem with hidden things. Somehow or another, they always got found out.

Part Three: Ashes on the water

Chapter 1

The re-naming

I had three dreams that woke me up, three times in the night. In the first one, we were swimming in the sea pool and everything happened the same as it had in real life. We ran down the beach, I put the ball on the edge and the fake dog poo behind it; they all jumped in, then Tressa jumped in and I went in after her.

We swam up and down fast to get warm. I threw the ball in, we played some games, and then Elspeth saw the dog poo. She screamed, Duncan said we'd have to bury it, and I went to pick it up. Only, in my dream, it wasn't fake. It was real dog poo, and my fingers squished right into it.

I pulled my hand away but it was covered in sticky, stinky poo. Everyone jumped back in disgust, and the smell was so bad I wanted to chuck. That's what woke me up, the smell. It made me retch.

When I went to sleep again, I seemed to go back into the same dream, running down the beach, jumping into the pool, everything the same as had happened in real life, only this time it wasn't the fake dog poo that I hid behind the ball—it was my cake.

We played some games, and then I went to pick my cake up, but it was all soft and squishy, so my hands sank right in. The cake collapsed and turned to mush, and both my hands were covered in it. 'That looks like sick,' Hamish said. Then I realised it was sick. It smelt like sick, and it was the sick-making smell that made me wake up.

The third dream was very short. I was standing on the edge of the pool, trying to force myself to jump in. But the water was icy blue, and I didn't want to. I looked across at Duncan and his eyes were the same colour, and all of a sudden they sucked me in like a giant whirlpool, whoosh! I was swept into that icy-cold blue, and I went right under. I was drowning.

I struggled and struggled to get back to the surface, until I woke up gasping for breath.

Duncan knew I was hiding something and he would keep staring me down until I cracked. Or maybe he would see into Tressa's mind like his ancestor the seer could do and force her to fess up, even if she didn't want to.

And I didn't think she did want to because the thing about big sisters is that although they might not always be nice to you themselves, they don't like it if someone else is mean to you. When Duncan had made me walk across the field to the south light, that was mean, and it was kind of Tressa's fault for telling.

One way or another, Duncan would find out I told Mum about the feast, and I couldn't stand the suspense. I just wanted to get it over with. So the next afternoon when we set off for the bothy, I put the cake in the bottom of the day-sack under the hats and gloves and mini-football. We were going to play some beach games and then have our meeting in the bothy. Duncan said it would be a review of our time in the Binding.

When we arrived, they were down at the water's edge, skipping stones. We played three-a-side, which worked surprisingly well, considering we had Milo.

He would normally be a handicap, but as Duncan, Hamish and Elspeth had never played before, they were nearly as bad as him.

Hamish and Elspeth went to prepare the bothy for the meeting, and the rest of us lay down on the dry sand at the top of the beach to wait until they were ready. When we finally went inside, I suddenly remembered the first time, how surprising and magical it had felt with the candles twinkling all around the edges and the fish-box chairs arranged in a circle round the driftwood table. Elspeth opening the box, her butterfly fingers fluttering over the black cloth and the big candle, and Hamish lighting it, and the way the flame lit up our faces. . .everything so perfect.

We made the circle, round and round, can't be unbound, and sat down in our places. Then Duncan asked each one of us to talk about something we had enjoyed during the time we had been in the Binding. Tressa remembered the day they took us to the wrecking rocks, and Milo the six candles, when he got to light his own. Hamish remembered the Fruits of Morna. 'That was really funny!' he said.

Elspeth remembered the swim in the pool, and Duncan the games night when we played charades and in-the-manner-of-the-word. I said I had enjoyed the feast on the beach, making the driftwood fire inside the circle of stones, and listening to Duncan's stories about his ancestors.

Duncan looked pleased about that. I teetered on the edge, not sure whether I could do it, but then I caught his eye and just plunged in.

'I made a cake for the feast, but I didn't bring it. I've brought it today.'

I lifted the Tupperware out of the day-sack, placed it on the edge of the table and took off the lid. The cake didn't look quite as glorious as it had when I first made it because it had slipped across to one side of the box on the way down to the beach and got a bit flattened, but still.

Milo's mouth dropped open.

'When did you make a cake?' he said.

'How did you do it without anyone noticing?' asked Hamish.

'I didn't.'

Duncan frowned at me. 'Are you telling on yourself?'

I hadn't thought of it in exactly those terms, but I supposed I was.

'If you are telling, you have to say the words,' said Duncan.

They all stared at me.

'All right.' My voice came out shaky. It didn't sound like me at all. 'I am the eyes and ears of the Lawmaker and I wish to make a report.'

The cake looked fluffy and light, every bit as good as the ones on the home-bakes stall at the school summer fete, even though it was a bit squashed.

'I wanted to bring something really nice, so I asked Mum to help me make a cake, and she asked what for, and I said because we were having a feast. That's all I said.'

Nobody spoke. They were waiting for Duncan. He stood up, and the rest of us stood up. Hamish handed him the Judgement and he put it on, but he still didn't say anything. He looked really angry, and he looked really big.

'I didn't want to steal food from my mum and Matt,' I said. 'I wasn't happy about it. I don't mind if everyone else wants to, but I just couldn't do it.'

Duncan glared at me. 'Have you ever helped yourself to a snack at home without asking?' His voice was as hard as nails.

'Well. . .yes. I suppose. If Mum's not around.'

'And is that stealing?'

'Well. . .no.'

'So you decided that on this particular occasion taking food without asking was stealing, and you took it upon yourself to tell your parents the secret business of the Binding.'

'No!' I said. 'I didn't tell them anything important, nothing about the laws and the candles and the meetings, none of that.'

'So you decide what's important now, do you? All on your own?'

'No! I just. . . I just. . .'

Duncan took a step back. The others did too. I stayed where I was, suddenly alone.

'The secrets of the Binding are not your secrets to tell,' Duncan said. 'They belong to us all. Being secret is what makes the Binding special. It's the root of everything we do; it's the thing that binds us together.'

He looked slowly round at the others, in the flickering candlelight.

'Who agrees with Jack?' he asked. 'Who thinks it's all right to tell the secrets of the Binding?'

No-one answered. Duncan turned to me.

'For the third time, Joker, you have broken the law of secrecy, which is the most sacred law of the Binding. This is your punishment—you are stripped of your name and I re-name you the Pretender. Do you know what that means?'

I shook my head. Tressa said it meant someone who wasn't a king but thought they should be, and wanted to fight the king for the throne.

'For one whole day, Pretender, you will be outside the circle; no-one will speak to you, except when grown-ups are around. The day after tomorrow, you will come back here, either to accept the rules and become part of the Binding again, or else to challenge me for the leadership.'

What kind of challenge? Did he mean an actual fight?

'If you challenge me and win, I will dissolve the Binding and you will make something else in its place, but if you lose you will be outside the circle forever.'

'But—'

'One more thing,' Duncan interrupted me. 'Between now and the day after tomorrow, if you tell any more of the business of the Binding to anyone outside, then there will be no coming back for you. Now take your cake and go.'

I stood for a moment outside the door, blinking in the daylight. The bright sun made my eyes water as I walked back to the house on my own, with the edge of the Tupperware pressing into my back.

I slipped behind the house to the sheds, sat down on a wrecked old chair, took out the Tupperware, opened it and broke off a big chunk of cake. If they didn't want it, that was their loss. But I did want it, and what's more I could have it, so I finished the first piece and broke off another.

I was full up and just picking off a few stray chocolate buttons when Tressa pushed the door open.

'I've been looking for you.' She came in, shutting the door behind her. 'Milo's playing in the old van.'

'You aren't supposed to be talking to me.'

She shrugged, cleared some boxes off an old kitchen stool and sat down.

'Why do you keep doing this?' she said. 'Don't you get it? The whole point about the Binding is it's secret. That's what makes it good.'

'Maybe for you.'

As I said it, I suddenly remembered how I'd felt when I'd told Mum about the bothy, kind of disappointed because now she knew, and definitely sure I didn't want to tell her anything else.

'OK,' I said, 'yes, I get it. I don't know why I asked about the cake.'

'So what are you going to do?'

I shrugged. 'We'll probably be leaving in a few days anyway.'

'Only if Mum gets her way.'

'She will.'

Tressa reached over and broke off a bit of cake. She ate it and took a bit more, with extra icing.

'This is really good!' she said. 'Look, it's just one day, and I'll still talk to you when Milo's not around. After that, come back to the bothy and say sorry. Grovel a bit. Tell Duncan you're going to toe the line. Then he'll let you be the Joker again.'

We hid the rest of the cake and went indoors. Mum and Matt were snuggled up on the sofa doing a crossword puzzle.

'Hello, you two!' said Matt.

'We've made a decision,' said Mum.

They smiled at each other.

'We're going to stay for the whole summer, just like we planned!'

Chapter 2

Outside looking in

Matt said it was the seal beach that did it. We were climbing up the hill, just the two of us, the next day, while Mum was finishing her book and Tressa and Milo were at the bothy.

'I don't think it was the seal beach,' I said. 'I think it was you.'

He stopped and smiled at me.

'And what about you, Jack—are you happy that we're staying?'

I said yes, I was. Then he asked me, 'What do you guys find to do here every day?'

I didn't tell him anything. Just playing, I said. Normal stuff.

It was a bright, clear day, with actual blue sky, and considering I was in exile I was in a good mood. Now that I knew we were staying, I knew what I had to do—go back and accept the rules—because there was no way I was going to spend the rest of the summer holidays out in the cold. And once I was back in, I would make sure I stayed right there, in the magic of the Binding.

Because it was magic, I could clearly see that now, from the outside looking in. Not just the candles and rituals and ceremonies, and all the things that happened in the bothy, but also the effect it had on everything else. Tressa was helpful in the house; she was nice to Matt—it even seemed as if she liked him.

Milo wasn't like a big baby any more, with that quivering bottom lip and hovering thumb, and tantrums every time he got separated from Nee-na. Also, he'd stopped whining if he had to walk somewhere or wait for dinner.

'Shall we carry on along the ridge like we did the first time?' asked Matt.

That felt like a lifetime ago. Now, looking down over the island from the triangulation point at the top, I recognised most of the coastline—the wrecking stones, the seal beach, the place where the Day Star ran aground. I realised we had still hardly explored inland at all.

Moving along the ridge until we could see down into the valley with the plantation of trees and the two Anderson Grounds made me feel curious. I knew Elspeth lived in the newer house at the very end of the track, but I didn't know who lived in the mysterious house among the trees.

So when we got home and found Tressa and Milo were still out, I decided to walk up the track towards the north end of the island, and do some exploring on my own. I passed lots of sheep, rabbits and birds and also, in the field beside Elspeth's house, a couple of goats, but not a single joke came into my head. Maybe that only happened when other people were around.

I heard shrieks coming from Elspeth's garden. Going nearer, I saw two girls filling plastic beakers with water from a bucket and throwing it at each other. They must have been playing for a while because they were both completely soaked.

One of them had to be Meggie, because she looked exactly like Elspeth, but smaller. She had the same light wispy hair and skinny body, but her voice was loud and lively, and when she laughed, she threw her head back in delight. I had never seen Elspeth laugh like that.

A woman came out of the house with a laundry basket, which she dropped beside the washing-line.

'Oh, hello!' she said, noticing me. 'Are you staying at Jean's house?'

She stopped pegging the washing and came over. She looked very friendly and smiley.

'Elspeth says you've been playing together, all of you. You must come over some time.'

I realised I had never had a friend before whose parents I didn't know, or whose house I hadn't been in.

'That would be nice,' I said.

'How are you enjoying your stay in Morna?'

Before I had a chance to answer, Meggie skidded on a patch of mud up near the house and fell flat on her face. She let out an ear-splitting scream.

'Sorry,' her mum said, over her shoulder, as she turned to go back and see to Meggie.

I didn't know whether it would be rude to go, but I also didn't want to get into a long conversation with Elspeth's mum in case I accidentally blabbed about the Binding, so I made my getaway and cut across the field towards the plantation.

Close to, I could see the trees were barely taller than me, tough-looking, old and gnarled, and leaning right over from the wind. Instead of making for the track, I climbed over the loose wire fence and went straight in among them. Although it was quite a still day, the leaves rustled on their wiry stems.

The ground underneath the trees was lumpy with roots and rabbit-holes, so I had to pick my way carefully. When I got within sight of the house, I stopped and slipped behind a tree.

It was a white-painted croft cottage like most of the houses around the jetty beach, but it looked different, nestling among the trees. There were bushes and flower-beds under the windows, full of tall nettles and weeds.

The sun on the windows made them like mirrors— all you could see in them was the trees outside. If someone lived here, I guessed it would be an old person, but it didn't really look as if anyone did.

Staying in the cover of the trees, I crept right round, to see the house from every angle. There was a barn with a few broken hay bales but no chickens. A yard with a byre but no horses or cows. A vegetable patch full of buttercups and brambles.

I'd come right back to where I had started and was just about to creep up to the windows and have a peep inside when I thought I saw something moving in the barn. I watched and waited, hiding among the trees.

Something touched the back of my leg and I jumped to the side in surprise. A black and white cat with yellow eyes looked calmly up at me, then curled itself around my legs, purring loudly.

'Go away!' I hissed. 'Shoo!'

It didn't look like a mangy stray, so someone must be around to feed it, and I didn't want it drawing attention to me. Plus I didn't like the feel of its heavy body leaning into my legs, and the way it carried on even after I'd tried to shoo it away.

I was bending down to give it a push and make it go, when a voice really close by exclaimed, 'Jack!'

I snapped upright and the cat strolled off to wrap itself around a different pair of legs—Elspeth's.

'What are you doing here?' she said.

'I didn't think anyone lived here,' I said. 'I was just exploring.'

If it had been Duncan, he would have said, 'Trespassing, more like. You don't go exploring in other people's private property!'

'No-one does live here,' she said. 'I just come up to feed Shadow.'

The cat, hearing its name, purred even louder and pressed even harder against her legs.

'Is it just you?' I asked, looking over my shoulder. If any of the others were around, they shouldn't see her talking to me. She nodded and turned to go back to the barn, tilting her head as if to say, 'Come with me.'

She had already put the cat food in a bowl, and she took it off the bench and put it on the floor. The cat gobbled it up, purring like an engine.

'No-one else comes up here,' Elspeth said. 'Do you want to see inside?'

I was more curious than ever now, and glad to hear that the house was empty and it would be all right to have a snoop around. I followed Elspeth across the yard to the back door. It wasn't locked, and I remembered Duncan telling us, 'Nobody locks their doors here.'

The back door went straight into the kitchen, which was like something from a museum. It had thin brown lino on the floor and cupboards that looked as if they'd been home-made and painted over a billion times. The sink was big and oblong, with metal legs instead of a cupboard underneath it.

There wasn't a cooker, but a big old range with four rings on the top and two ovens. Everything looked exactly as if somebody still lived there—plates and cups stacked on the wooden draining-board, tea-towels draped over a string to dry, saucepans hanging from a beam—but everything felt cold.

'My granny and grandpa built this house,' Elspeth said. 'It was the first Anderson Ground.'

Of course! Anderson was Elspeth's surname. That was why her grandparents' and parents' houses were both called Anderson Ground.

'Grandpa planted all the trees. I don't really remember him, because he died when I was three.'

She looked as nervous as a rabbit and I didn't want to make trouble for her.

'I think I should go. I mean, you're not even supposed to be talking to me.'

'But the thing is, you were right!' she said. 'Taking things from your parents without asking is stealing.'

I was going to argue it like Duncan had, but she hadn't finished.

'It feels wrong to always do as you're told and be good, and not argue when your parents are around. It's like tricking them, or lying or something. And also, it's wrong to be rude, and we're being rude to you, by not talking.'

I said it didn't matter, I didn't mind. I'd had a nice morning with Matt and anyway it was only for one day.

'But still, I'm sorry,' she said. 'It wasn't like this when Fin was here. Fin wasn't scared of Duncan. But now Fin's gone.'

Chapter 3

Seeing Elspeth

Shadow wound himself round Elspeth's legs, purring loudly, until she picked him up.

'Poor thing,' she said. 'He misses Granny. We've tried to make him live with us now she isn't here any more, but he keeps coming back.'

She led the way into the other downstairs room, which felt slightly cosier, but still as cold. There was lino on the floor like in the kitchen, but with a square carpet in the middle and two stiff-looking armchairs, one on each side of the fireplace. Above the mantelpiece, a scenes-of-Scotland calendar was hanging on a pin, still open on the January picture of a big hill covered in snow.

I could imagine Elspeth and her granny sitting in that room, talking. They would be eating those cardboardy biscuits in cellophane bags that they sold in the shop, and drinking milk that came from the cow in the byre.

Elspeth would ask about her grandpa, and her granny would tell her stories from the old times, and it was weird, because in my imagination Elspeth in her granny's house felt solid and real, where in the bothy she seemed like someone who almost wasn't there: a trick of the candlelight, a whisper on the air.

I followed her upstairs to the bedroom she or her little sister Meggie or their cousin Fin used to sleep in whenever one of them stayed. It was so tiny that an ordinary bed couldn't fit in there, so Elspeth's dad had built one specially, like a wide shelf with a mattress. There were three wooden boxes underneath where Elspeth, Meggie and Fin once kept some of their clothes and games, but they were empty now.

'Is this your granny?' I asked, pointing to the photo in the little silver picture-frame on the bedside table.

Elspeth nodded.

'It was the first picture I ever took with the camera she gave me last Christmas. That's why it's a bit blurry, but Granny liked it. She said you couldn't see her wrinkles.'

The cat wriggled in her arms and jumped down, disappearing through the open door—now you see me, now you don't. I could understand why they called him Shadow. We found him again in the other bedroom, rolling on the bed.

This room was much bigger, with a long chest of drawers covered in photos, some yellowing black and white, and others bright and new. Elspeth showed me her grandpa, leaning on his spade among the baby trees, and her great-auntie Hannah who went to Australia.

'This one's Auntie Lou and Uncle Fraser,' she said, 'and that's Finlay when he was little.'

There was a school photo at the back, taken last year, with Duncan, Hamish, Elspeth and Finlay and their teacher sitting on chairs behind five younger children, cross-legged on the floor. Elspeth said that was the whole school and playgroup. She pointed out Meggie and her friend, Christa, giggling at each other, beside three even younger ones, gawping at the camera.

'Granny didn't like Duncan,' Elspeth said, still looking at the photo.

'Why not?'

She glanced at me, as if she was making up her mind whether to tell me.

'Granny used to say she could see colours round people, and Duncan's colours were very dark.'

I remembered Hamish saying, 'Yes, but your granny was a bit mad, wasn't she?'

'Do you like Duncan?' I asked.

She looked at the photo again.

'He isn't the kind of person you like,' she said. 'But you want to see him; you want to listen to him and be around him—I don't know.'

She said she couldn't explain, but she didn't need to.

'And what about Fin?' I asked. In the picture, he looked taller than Duncan, Hamish and Elspeth, but that might just have been because he was sitting up straight, very smiley and confident.

'It was always Hamish and Duncan—they were best friends—and Fin and me, but all four of us played together as well because there wasn't anyone else our age to play with.'

Her voice seemed stronger, here in her grandmother's house, and less like a silvery whisper.

'It was Hamish and Duncan who found the bothy and made it into a den. That's what it was in the beginning, just a den. Somewhere we could all go and play.'

Elspeth said Duncan and Fin always used to argue—like their teacher said, they were both 'strong characters'—so it wasn't surprising when they fell out over Duncan's ideas about creating a secret club.

'He wanted to be the leader and make the rules, but Fin told him to stop being an idiot.'

'I bet Duncan didn't like that.'

'They had a massive argument, but Duncan wouldn't let it go. He said we were going to do it anyway, whether Fin liked it or not. Nothing happened after that though, and we thought it had all blown over, but then one day when we went to the bothy, Duncan had got there first and he'd made the driftwood table and fish-box chairs.

'He told us to sit down and we all did, because we were curious to see what he had in mind. Fin played along, treating it all like a joke.

'When Duncan gave us our names, and Fin was the Warrior, he laughed and said that was about right.

He wasn't going to let Duncan push him around.

'And he didn't. If Duncan tried to make him do anything he didn't want to in the Binding, he just laughed it off.'

I could guess that from his picture.

'It was really good at first.' Elspeth sighed. 'Duncan turned out to be brilliant at making up ceremonies and stories, and he could get all kinds of things from the hotel store cupboards without anyone noticing. It felt kind of natural for him to be the leader.'

He could be bossy, of course, and tetchy when Fin wouldn't do what he decreed. Once or twice they'd nearly come to blows. 'Do you want to be in charge, is that it?' Duncan would shout, squaring up to Fin. 'Do you think you could do it better than me?'

Then he'd turn on Elspeth and Hamish, saying, 'What about you? Do you think Fin could do it better?'

'And the fact was, we didn't,' Elspeth said. 'Not really.'

Elspeth sat down on the bed next to Shadow, and stroked his ears. I sat down too. I could see that talking about Fin was upsetting her, but I really wanted to know what had happened.

'Well, one day, Duncan got the idea for the Judgement. Before that, he'd told us what to do and Fin mostly hadn't done it, so he said we needed punishments. Fin told him he'd lost the plot if he thought any of us were going to put up with that, and Duncan went completely mental.

'He said Fin was always trying to spoil everything, and enough was enough. I thought they were going to have an actual fight, which would have been terrible because Fin isn't as strong as Duncan, or as aggressive, but Duncan suddenly went all calm. "We're going to sort this out once and for all," he said, and then he walked out.'

'We didn't go to the bothy for a whole week after that, but the next time we were there, everything felt different. You could tell something had happened. Duncan was acting weird, and Fin seemed moody and bad-tempered, which wasn't like him at all.'

Elspeth picked Shadow up off the blanket and tried to cuddle him, but he struggled free, jumped down onto the floor and shot out the door. For a few moments, she just sat there, staring after him.

'Fin left soon after that,' she said, her eyes still fixed on the open door. 'I thought the reason he wasn't his

176

normal self those last few weeks was because he was upset about leaving. I mean, he loved Morna as much as I do.

'But the day before he left, he told me he was glad to be going. He said, "Be careful of Duncan. Don't cross him."

'That's why I said it to you, when you first came,' she added.

Nobody did cross Duncan any more after Fin had gone. Hamish was best mates with him, and Elspeth was wary because of what Fin had said. In a way, that made the Binding even stronger and more magical. As Duncan moved fully into his power, he seemed to have even better ideas.

'It was exciting,' Elspeth said. 'He made us do hard things like the leap, and told us scary stories about places like the wreckers' beach, which came back in our dreams.

'We weren't keen on some of the things we had to do, like the rules of how to behave at home, but that was part of the Binding, and we got swept up in it.

'Me and Hamish never crossed him and never had to do a punishment, but then you came, and I warned you, and you didn't listen, and he made you go into the bonxies' nesting ground. Then you crossed him again, and now we can't talk to you, and everything feels wrong.'

'Are you saying I've spoilt the Binding? I didn't mean to.'

'You didn't spoil it,' she said. 'You reminded me of Fin.'

We came out into the sunny back yard. Shadow was hunting in the gap between the outbuildings. Elspeth said he was a good mouser—the trouble was he'd take anything. Frogs, slow-worms, baby birds. . .once he'd even tried to kill a hedgehog.

'Duncan says that's just his nature, and nature is cruel.'

I suddenly thought of the flowers flying up into the air as Duncan beat the nettles with his stick, and the scared little chick, that time, in his fist.

'You reminded me of lots of things,' Elspeth said, going back to what we were talking about before. 'When you came, we started playing again, in the pool, on the beach and in the bothy, and I remembered what it was like before the Binding, when the bothy was just a den and there weren't any rules.'

She sighed. 'I wish we could go back to how it was before.'

'You could just leave,' I said.

'No, I couldn't.' She shook her head. 'If I left, I would be completely on my own.'

I tried to imagine what it would be like to live here, not for a summer, but forever, with only Duncan and Hamish your own age, and nobody else to play with. How would it feel if your best friend had moved away, when there was no-one else around who could become your new best friend and stop those two from walking all over you?

We left the yard, walked round the end of the house and started down the track between the trees. Neither of us said anything until we reached the junction and were going our separate ways.

'Anyway, it's not your problem,' she said. 'You'll be leaving and going back to your own life soon.'

I watched her run up the track towards her house, as light and quick on her feet as Shadow. Now you see me, now you don't. She was disappearing again, like she did in the Binding, where she looked no more than a trick of the light and sounded no more than a whisper.

Chapter 4

One word and it's over

I walked back down towards Jean's house on my own. There were sheep nibbling the grass at the edge of the track, sometimes ambling across in front of me, their raggy wool dangling beneath their bellies.

When we first came to the island, I was actually wary of the sheep. They were silly and jumpy, but there were lots of them, and you never knew which way they were going to run. I used to try to avoid them but now I walked calmly through the middle and they cleared the way.

'It's not your problem,' Elspeth had said. There was nothing to stop me accepting the Binding under Duncan, enjoying the magic of more strange events and adventures, and then going home to my normal life, a thousand miles away.

'It's not your problem.' She was right. So why would I take Duncan's challenge?

I suddenly thought of Jenson Powell. I had hardly noticed him until we were in Year 5 because he didn't use to play football, but then Arthur, Marc and Truan suddenly had it in for him. No-one knew what he'd done to deserve it, but they kept calling him names and kicking his legs and stuff like that, and if anyone tried to stick up for him, they got the same treatment.

Not that anyone did much, after the first few days. No-one stuck up for him, including me. I didn't stick up for him because he wasn't really my friend, and that meant it wasn't my problem.

The longer it went on, the more he got that not-there look, like Elspeth in the Binding—sort of empty and sunken in. Then there was this day when Mrs Ford was away and we were waiting for the supply teacher, and everyone was getting bored. It got noisy, and Arthur, Marc and Truan pinned Jenson down, pulled off one of his shoes and started throwing it to each other.

They threw it to each other and then to other kids. Jenson kept trying to get it back but he knew he didn't have a hope. Arthur, Marc and Truan were laughing, and soon everyone was laughing, and the noise brought Mr Carter marching down from his office to find out what was going on.

He told us we should all be ashamed of ourselves, and I was ashamed, especially after it came to light what Jenson had actually done to get picked on in the first place. What he'd done was he had cried in the dinner line, which anyone would do if they had a really ill sister like he did.

Trying to shove that thought out of my head as I walked along was making me feel hungry, so as soon as I got back I went to the shed to have some of my secret cake. Tressa was there, waiting for me.

'Where have you been?' she demanded. 'Me and Milo got back from the bothy ages ago.'

'Well I'm not going to sit around and mope, am I?' I said, though that was obviously what she thought

I'd be doing, just because I wasn't allowed at the meeting.

I broke off a bit of cake, and passed the Tupperware to Tressa.

'So where were you?'

'Exploring,' I said. 'What did you do at the bothy?'

'We had a fire and toasted marshmallows on sticks. Duncan got Elspeth to read from her pages about some of the feasts and celebrations they had before we came.'

'That sounds good.'

'It'll be even better tomorrow, when you're back.'

I finished my cake and picked a corner of icing off the bit that was left in the box.

'What?' she said, when I didn't say anything.

'I'm thinking of taking Duncan's challenge.'

She laughed and then, catching my eye, stopped laughing.

'You can't be serious!'

'Why not?'

'Well for one thing, he's bigger and cleverer than you. You won't win.'

'Thanks for your support.'

I put the lid back on the Tupperware and hid it again. Tressa said why should she support me? She didn't want me to challenge Duncan. She liked the Binding. It was amazing, and we would never find anything like it anywhere else in the world.

'You're going to ruin everything,' she said. 'Not just for us, either. Think about that. We'll be going home at the end of the holidays, but Duncan, Hamish and Elspeth will still be here.'

'Yes, well, that's the point.'

I told her what Elspeth had told me about how it used to be her and Fin, and Duncan and Hamish, two pairs of best friends, only now that Fin wasn't there any more, it was Hamish and Duncan, as thick as thieves.

'What's this got to do with the Binding?' said Tressa.

'Elspeth says the Binding was better when Fin was there because he stood up to Duncan, and they didn't do stealing from their parents and stuff. She doesn't want to do it, but she's scared. If she crosses Duncan, she thinks she'll be out on her own, and there's no-one else here for her to be friends with.'

Tressa frowned.

'That's not our problem though, is it?'

I told Tressa about the house in the trees, how it had belonged to Elspeth's granny who died, and Elspeth was really missing her. First she lost Fin and then she lost her granny, and she was really unhappy.

'Imagine if our granny lived next door, and we could go back and forth to her house across the fields whenever we liked, and stay over if we wanted, and then one day, she dies and she's gone forever. No-one there. Just a cold empty house.'

Milo appeared in the doorway.

'Are you talking?' he asked, suspiciously.

'Of course not,' Tressa said. 'That would be against the rules, right?'

'I think you were talking,' Milo muttered.

Tressa got up and steered him out of the shed. 'Why don't you give me a ride in your van?'

She didn't bring it up again. You could tell she was thinking I wouldn't do it anyway, what with having the backbone of a jellyfish and everything. I actually didn't think I'd do it either. I wasn't even certain that I wanted to.

I still didn't think I'd do it as we walked down to the bothy beach the following afternoon. It was sunny, the tide was right out and I had a tennis ball in my pocket. We could have a game after the meeting. We could have a brilliant time and then go home for tea, all talking to each other.

Duncan and the others were sitting on the grass outside the bothy. Milo did his solemn duty of opening the door for everyone, but Duncan told me to wait outside and then he shut the door on me himself. I just got a glimpse of the candles on the floor, the fish-box seats and the driftwood table.

I thought he was making a point, and in a few minutes he would send his Page to open the door and let me in. But he didn't, and I was left sitting there on my own, wondering what they could possibly be doing inside that was taking so long.

I couldn't go down the beach and skip stones in case they called me in, but I didn't want to sit around outside not doing anything for ages either. I was actually feeling quite tetchy by the time Milo opened the door.

He closed the door again behind me, shutting the darkness in.

'Don't sit down,' Duncan said.

I stood behind my fish-box seat and they all looked up at me, their faces yellow in the candlelight.

'Pretender, do you accept the rules of the Binding and do you accept me as your Lawmaker? Are you ready to give up the name Pretender and become the Joker again?'

I don't know! I need time! Don't push me!

Tressa gave me her best for-goodness-sake-get-on-with-it-and-stop-messing-around look. Milo and Hamish, on either side of Duncan, were trying to stare me down like him. Elspeth didn't meet my eye. She looked so small and sad.

'No.'

There was a stunned silence. 'Don't cross him,' Fin had said. Elspeth's granny said all his colours were dark. I thought, *What have I done?*

Duncan had a face like thunder, and when he spoke his voice came out much louder than usual.

'You will go away from here and not return. In the next few days, I will offer you a challenge, as we agreed. If you win, I will keep my word and close the Binding—but if you lose, the Binding will continue, and therefore you must agree to protect it in the meantime by honouring the rule of secrecy.'

He nodded to Milo, who jumped up and opened the door. As I walked out, I suddenly realised that whatever happened, I would never go back there again. Even if the Binding continued, I was excluded forever.

One little word, that was all I had said, and now it was over.

Chapter 5

Running in the mist

Obviously, Tressa really did stop talking to me after that. She was furious. But as luck would have it, we had a new family project to take our minds off things. We were learning to dance.

Every summer, there was a ceilidh in the hall which was the big event of the year. Everyone went, young and old, and people who had once lived on Morna came back to visit for the ceilidh weekend. Jean from next door went if she was on the island, along with several other bird-watchers from England and the

Scottish mainland who had houses there. All the hotel guests were invited too.

Mum said that if we were going to the ceilidh we had to at least know some of the dances, and she could teach us one or two such as the Gay Gordons that she'd learnt a thousand years ago when she was at school. We found some Scottish dance music on the laptop, so we were set.

By the evening of the ceilidh we knew three dances, but we soon discovered that dancing in a hall full of people who know what they're doing is nothing like pushing back the furniture and plodding through the steps at home.

They stamped and marched, leapt and skipped; they spun each other round so fast that if you weren't careful you got trampled on, even in the dances you could more or less keep up in. When it came to the reels, which none of us knew how to do at all, we got swept up and carried along by smiling strangers, steering us round and shouting instructions above the noise of the fiddles and the squeezebox.

It was hot and sweaty in the crowded little hall and no-one sat out except three really old ladies and a baby asleep in its carry-cot. There was just time between dances to grab a glass of lemonade from the drinks table near the door if you were thirsty, and that's what I was doing when Duncan came up beside me and put a scrap of paper in my hand.

'Bothy, 9 o'clock,' I read, before pushing it down into my pocket.

I thought it would be some kind of meeting and everyone would all know. They'd probably arranged it the last time they were at the bothy. So I planned to wait until the others left the ceilidh and follow them down. But it got nearer and nearer to nine o'clock, and they all still seemed to be there.

Except, I suddenly noticed, Duncan. He must have slipped out on his own when no-one was looking. Tressa was busy trying to explain about stripping the willow to Milo by telling him it was like cars weaving in and out on the motorway, but he still wasn't getting it. Hamish was dancing with one of his aunties and Elspeth was helping Meggie with her shoelaces.

None of them were meeting each other's eyes or looking out for a chance to slip away, and none of them were watching for me leaving. I realised it wasn't going to be a meeting of the Binding at nine o'clock—it was just Duncan and me.

Of all the times he could have chosen, why now? I was enjoying the ceilidh and I didn't want to miss any of it. *Oh, I get it*, I thought. *That's why it has to be now.*

I thought, *I'm not going.* But then, if I didn't, I might not have another chance. Duncan's challenge could be a one-time only offer. So I went to the drinks table and pretended I was looking for a clean glass. From there to the door was only a few steps, and nobody noticed me leave.

It was darker than it should have been at that time in the evening because a thick mist had come in during the afternoon, completely blocking out the sky. No sunset, no moonrise, no stars, just this soft eerie fog soaking up the lights from the hall like a sponge. Outside that halo of yellow light, I couldn't see more than a few feet in front of me, so it was lucky I knew the way to the bothy like the back of my hand.

I made my way up the track, with sometimes a house suddenly looming up, or a barn or a garden wall. I had to keep telling myself that, as Mum and Matt had said, there wasn't any danger on a small island like this; it was safe to be out and about on your own.

I didn't want to leave the track but I forced myself, following the fence down across the field to the shore, stumbling over dips and tussocks. By the time I got to the sea it was too late to turn back, and I picked my way along the coast to the bothy beach. So long as I stuck to the track, the fence, the shoreline, at least I couldn't get lost.

The fog was rolling and swirling across the sand. I couldn't see the water but I could hear the soft lapping of the waves. I was expecting to see flickering firelight or candlelight inside the bothy when I got close enough, but the windows were completely dark.

I was standing there wondering what to do next when a voice behind me said, 'You're late.'

He was standing further up the beach, a dark featureless figure in the fog, like a ghost. I stayed rooted to the spot, and he came crunching across the stones towards me.

'Are you ready for the challenge?'

Now he was close by, I could see his face and that hard bright shine in his eyes that he always got when he was excited about something. I nodded in a way that I hoped looked calm and confident. I didn't say anything because I was sure my voice would give me away. Besides, my teeth seemed to be locked together, like when you're so cold you're past the chattering stage.

I *was* cold, too. The mist had soaked my hair, slicking it down onto my head and falling in big droplets onto the neck and shoulders of my sweatshirt. I wanted to say, 'Let's forget about all this and go back to the dance.'

'The challenge is a race,' Duncan said, 'from here to the next beach, along the bottom of the cliffs.'

A race? Suddenly, things were looking up. When you're a footballer, you do a lot of training. Speed, stamina and agility, that's the name of the game. Duncan hardly even knew how to play football and he'd definitely never done any training. He was stocky to the point of overweight, and he didn't know how fit I was. He had chosen the wrong challenge. He had made a mistake!

'All right,' I said. 'Just to be clear, it's the beach with all the driftwood?'

He nodded. We'd explored all the way along this piece of coast so I knew exactly what it was like, mostly low grassy banks above a sloping platform of rock, with little pebbly inlets and gullies. As I remembered it, the next beach wasn't very far.

'Ready? Go!'

The rocks were wet and slippery, and we couldn't see far in front of us in the mist. Down onto the first patch of pebbles we went, with me keeping slightly ahead, easily holding the lead. Carefully now, on the smooth wet rock, then more pebbles, and then rock again, with the sea slapping against the hard rock and swooshing amongst the pebbles, invisible in the mist.

I could hear him puffing and panting behind me, then a sudden gasp as he slipped and fell down. I turned to see if he was hurt, but he got straight up again and I thought, *No, you're not catching me up!* I picked up my speed.

Rounding the headland, I was expecting to see the beach, but it was just more rocks and stones. It must be round the next one, I thought, not stopping, keeping it steady.

I couldn't hear Duncan any more; he must be miles behind. This was so easy! Towards the next headland the rocky ledge was narrower and I could see the water lapping along the edge, higher than I had expected it to be. The tide must be coming in.

Instead of the beach, I came down onto another patch of pebbles, but I wasn't tired. I pushed on. It was like when you go up a hill and you keep thinking you're coming to the top, and when you get there, you see that the hill carries on.

Again and again, I thought I was going to see the beach round the next corner, only to find another stretch of rocks and stones. But then, all of a sudden, I was there! I ran down onto the sand, yelling in triumph.

This beach was steeper than the bothy beach, and narrower. It made a V shape into the cliffs, which were higher and steeper. Heaps of driftwood were piled up along the top of the beach at the foot of the cliffs.

I waited, listening hard. I couldn't hear Duncan clambering over the rocks or trying to catch his breath, although the fog was full of sounds. I heard the waves slapping and sighing in and out on the sand, and the gulls further out, screaming to each other over the sea.

I sat on a railway sleeper that had been washed up long ago and was half-buried in sand. Before long, the waves were nearly up to my feet and I had to move.

Where was he?

I walked back towards the end of the beach, having to stay near the bottom of the cliff now because the tide was so far in. I peered into the mist, but I didn't see Duncan. What I saw was the sea, washing over the rocks I had run over just a short time before.

I felt sick. I felt stupid too. There was a reason why the driftwood on this beach had never been collected by the islanders, and that was because the beach was difficult to get to. The cliffs were higher and there was no path down, and the only other way onto the beach was along the rocky shore, which was cut off at the high tide.

Where was Duncan?

A wave broke over my feet and I had to retreat back up to the very top of the beach. I looked up into the V of the cliffs, and there he was, looking down.

'Say I'm the leader,' he shouted. 'Say you accept the laws of the Binding!'

Not a single soul knew where we were.

'Say it!' he shouted again.

Chapter 6

A really big secret

Duncan was holding something in his hand, shaking it at me. It was a coil of rope.

'Say I'm the leader!'

The cliffs were steep but not sheer. They weren't like a slab of solid stone, but rocky and rubbly, with patches of grass and earth. They were no higher than the climbing wall in the Mill Street gym and I might have been able to climb up if the weather had been dry, but the mist had made everything slippery.

'Be confident.' That's what Dad had said the first time we went to the gym. 'But if you can't be confident, don't climb.'

'Throw down the rope!' I yelled, suddenly finding my voice. 'Stop being an idiot!'

'I can wait,' he said. 'Shame you can't.'

The sea was lifting the driftwood up from the sand and swilling it around. If it got closer to where I was standing, I was afraid a big wave might fling it at my legs and knock me over.

I reached up, testing for firm footholds and handholds but the first one I tried fell away.

'I could leave you here!' shouted Duncan.

There had to be a way. I walked along the bottom of the cliff as far as I could in both directions, while Duncan shouted down at me about how I wouldn't win and I was nothing but a stupid outsider who didn't understand anything.

'If you think I wouldn't leave you down there, think again!'

I made a few more attempts at climbing the cliff, but each time, either my foot slipped or the surface gave way, sending down a shower of rocks and earth.

Even if I managed to get some of the way, the risk of falling was too great.

Then I heard something, very faintly, in the distance. It was Tressa's voice, calling our names. Hamish joined in, then Elspeth, and then they all called our names together. Duncan and me both stood stock still, him at the top of the cliff and me on the beach below, listening. Minute by minute, they seemed to be getting closer.

I cupped my hands around my mouth and shouted back. 'Tressa! Elspeth! Hamish! Over here!' I kept shouting, so they could hear where we were, even though they couldn't see anything in the fog.

Duncan suddenly disappeared and then came back again. He threw the end of the rope down over the cliff and it dangled close to where I was standing.

'It's OK,' he shouted. 'I've tied it to a fence-post. It'll hold your weight. Don't worry!' His voice sounded completely different, not mocking and threatening any more, but like a rescuing hero. It was slightly louder too, as if he was playing to an audience, and straight away, the audience shouted back.

'Duncan! Jack!'

Elspeth, Tressa and Hamish sounded very close now. 'Where are you?'

I got a grip on the rope and gave it a tug. It felt firm, but I didn't trust Duncan. I wanted to wait until the others were there before I tried to climb up. I kept shouting their names.

'It's all right—I've tied it!' Duncan yelled down at me. 'What are you waiting for?'

Then I saw what I was waiting for. Tressa's face peering down at me through the fog, with Elspeth and Hamish on either side.

'How did you get down there?' Tressa cried.

Before I could answer, Hamish yelled, 'Watch out!'

A big wave was rolling towards me, covered in floating driftwood. I grabbed the rope and got my feet up off the sand just in time. Then hand over hand, using the rope to take my weight, I felt for toe-holds with my feet and worked my way slowly up, until I got near enough for Hamish and Duncan to reach down and haul me over the edge onto the soaking grass.

'How could you be so stupid?' Tressa said. 'That was really dangerous.'

I was still on all fours, trying to catch my breath.

'He tricked me,' I managed to say, between gasps.

They all looked at Duncan.

'It's not my fault if he's stupid,' he said.

I struggled to my feet. 'He said it was the challenge. It was supposed to be a race, but it was a trap.'

Hamish looked confused. He said to Duncan, 'He could have drowned.'

'I brought the rope, didn't I?' Duncan snapped back.

The fog was pouring up over the cliff on an updraft of air, swirling around us, drenching our hair and eyelashes, covering our clothes with tiny droplets of water. Hamish took a step away from Duncan, as if he wanted to get a better look at him, or as if he was seeing him for the first time.

Elspeth said, 'This is what happened between you and Fin! Isn't it?'

Duncan had his back to the cliff, with the four of us penning him in. He looked angry and mean, like a rat in a trap.

'Answer me!' Elspeth said, in a voice that wasn't a whisper any more, but strong and clear above the wind.

'Your precious Fin was stupid too.' He spat the words at Elspeth but she didn't flinch.

'You drove him away,' she said. 'You made him feel glad he was leaving.'

Duncan turned to Hamish to back him up. 'Fin was spoiling the Binding, right? He had to be stopped.'

But Hamish shook his head. 'You don't get it, do you? Someone could have got killed.'

'My brother could have got killed!' yelled Tressa, suddenly making a lunge for Duncan. I grabbed her and pulled her towards me, scared they might both go over the cliff. We could hear the sea crashing against the rocks below, though we couldn't see it in the mist.

Duncan took his chance. He dived through the gap where Tressa had been, and ran off into the darkness. Nobody moved to go after him.

My legs went weak and I had to sit down, even though the grass was soaking wet.

'How did you know where we were?' I asked.

Crouching down beside me, Tressa said she'd noticed that I wasn't at the dance when she got fed up with Milo trampling on her feet and started looking for someone to take over. She told Elspeth and Hamish, and they realised that none of them had seen Duncan for a while either.

'We knew it must be the challenge, so we went down to the bothy,' said Elspeth. 'You weren't there, but as we started coming back, Tressa said she heard something, so we stopped to listen.'

'It sounded like someone shouting, but we couldn't really tell,' said Tressa. 'It could have been a sheep that got stuck in a fence, or even seagulls calling, or maybe it was nothing and we imagined it in the mist.

'We decided to go a little way towards where we thought it was coming from, but we couldn't see two metres in front of us, so we all held hands and picked our way across the field.'

As they moved nearer, the sound became clearer, so they knew it was people shouting, and very soon, they knew who.

'So we started shouting your names,' Elspeth said, 'and by then I thought I knew where we were going. Towards the driftwood beach, not the long way around the coast but directly, as the crow flies.'

'What are we going to do now?' Hamish asked.

'We should probably go back to the ceilidh before they send out a search party,' said Elspeth. She offered me her hand and I let her pull me up.

We followed the stream inland and hit the track between Anderson Ground and Jean's house. Mum had left the porch light on but there was obviously no-one home yet, so we carried on down to the hall.

We dived into the toilets before we went in, slipped out of our sweatshirts to shake the droplets of water off and dried our hair under the hand-driers. But Mum still greeted us with, 'Have you been outside? You look soaked and frozen!' Matt said all kids loved running around in the dark, and he was probably right—Milo would definitely have been cross with us for going without him if he hadn't been busy teaching Meggie his made-up 'London reel'.

I didn't want to dance any more. My head felt fuzzy and my legs felt weak. None of us wanted to dance, so it was just as well that the band was packing up. Some people stayed to clear away the leftover food and sweep the floor, while the rest of us scrabbled for our things in the jumble of coats and poured out into the night.

It was properly dark by then, and we had to point our torches at the ground because if we pointed them straight ahead all we could see was luminous fog. There was a crowd of us at first, but gradually people filtered off as they reached their own houses.

Me, Tressa, Hamish and Elspeth were walking in a huddle at the back, not really talking but still wanting to be on our own. Mum stopped and waited for us to catch up.

'Where did you get to?' she asked. 'I think you were gone a long time.'

She knew something had happened.

'We went to the beach,' I said, which wasn't a lie because we did go to a beach, only not the one she assumed, the one with the jetty.

'It was spooky in the fog,' Tressa said, trying to make it sound like a great game.

Elspeth and Hamish played along. 'We all held hands so we wouldn't get lost.' 'We had a race along the water's edge.' 'We watched the tide come in.'

Not one of us told on Duncan. It wasn't a plan, just an instinct. We kept his secret, which was a big secret, like the one that Fin had been keeping. Only this time it wouldn't be one person's word against another's if we should ever decide to tell.

Now everyone else had the power, and Duncan had none.

Chapter 7

Ashes on the water

By morning, the mist had cleared and me, Tressa and Milo walked down to the bothy in the sunshine. We were meeting Hamish and Elspeth, but none of us had any idea what we were going to do when we got there.

'It'll be like when we first found the bothy,' Tressa said. 'We thought it was a den, and now I suppose it is.'

I suddenly remembered coming down onto the beach our very first day and seeing the bothy huddled under the cliff; Tressa's hand on the door handle; me saying we shouldn't go in. Then the darkness inside, the fish-box seats and the driftwood table.

I remembered how it felt as our eyes got used to the dark and we found the curious circles of things in the corners, the shelves in the wall, the plate and the knife, the row of tiny skulls and finally the locked tin box with *Privite—keep out* written on it. Tressa's eyes lighting up as she realised it was a child's writing and that meant this must be a den.

But this time, it wasn't like the first time at all. The door was open, and everything had gone. The makeshift chairs and table, the shelves and all the things on them, the candles, the pile of driftwood beside the hearth, the fishing net with all the things in it, the shell circles and the line of skulls. The bothy had been stripped bare.

As we stood there in the gloom, trying to take it in, a shadow blocked the light from the door and Hamish walked in, closely followed by Elspeth.

'Where is everything?' she said.

We looked at each other and shrugged. Then Hamish said, 'I think I know.' He led us back outside and down to the circle of big stones where we'd built the fire for the Feast of the Ancestors. There was a heap of new ash in the middle, with charred bits of wood from the fish-boxes leaning in from the sides.

Blackened shells and pebbles broke the surface of the ash, with scraps of string from the fishing net and empty tea-light foils. In the middle was the tin box, all twisted and burnt out.

Hamish picked up one of the pieces of wood and poked at the ashes.

'It's cold,' he said. 'Duncan must have done this last night.'

I tried to imagine Duncan coming back, deep in the darkness, making the fire, dragging the driftwood table down the beach, throwing all the things from the bothy into the flames. Had he been in a furious rage? Or had he been sad, because it was the end of the Binding?

Elspeth sat down, and then we all sat down around the dead fire as if it was still alight, gazing into the ashes as if they were flames. It was like we were waiting for someone to come and tell us what to do.

'I suppose we could start again,' said Hamish. 'We could find some more fish-boxes and make a new table.'

I noticed a scrap of black cloth, snagged on a charred bit of wood, all that was left of the Judgement.

'Maybe we should look for a new place,' said Elspeth.

'Yes, but where?'

I tried to think of the many old sheds and buildings we'd seen on the island, but they all seemed to either have no roof or no door or no glass in the windows, or else they were too close to people's houses. Then I had a brainwave.

'What about your granny's house?'

They looked at me as if I'd gone mad, so I said to Elspeth. 'You go up there on your own. Why couldn't we all go?'

'It couldn't be secret,' she said. 'My mum and dad would have to know.'

'But it would still be our own place,' said Hamish. 'They wouldn't be there.'

'Would they let us, though?' Tressa asked. 'What about safety and all that?'

'The electricity's turned off, but it isn't dark like the bothy so we wouldn't need candles.'

'And it's just across the field from your house so we could easily get help if we had any problems.'

'Yes but. . .I don't know.' Elspeth frowned. 'What would Granny think?'

'She loved having you there when she was alive,' said Hamish. 'Why should it be any different now?'

Elspeth considered it. She slowly nodded her head.

'Granny would like to have all of us in her house. She'd want Meggie to come too,' she said.

Milo jumped up like a jack-in-the-box and did a little dance of excitement at the thought of Elspeth's little sister joining in. We looked up and there behind him, coming down the beach, was Duncan.

He came straight to where we were sitting. You might have expected him to be sheepish, ashamed even, about what had happened the night before, but Duncan didn't do sheepish and ashamed. It was the same as after my punishment with the birds— something had been done that had to be done, and that was that. No inquests, no regrets.

'I promised I would finish the Binding and I've done what I can.' He gestured towards the cold ash inside the ring of stones. 'Now, if you agree, I think we should have a closing ceremony.'

He actually said, 'If you agree'! He looked at us, one after the other, fixing us for a moment with those

210

piercing blue eyes before moving on, and when he saw that we all agreed, he took off his backpack and undid the string.

He took out a big tin camping mug and filled it with ash from the fire.

'Page, for the last time, please serve the Lawmaker and carry this.'

Milo looked at the rest of us to check it was OK, before he took the mug, and then we all followed in a procession down the beach onto the hard sand near the water's edge under the sparkling sun.

Duncan told us to take off our shoes and socks. He rolled up his trouser bottoms; the rest of us didn't need to because we were wearing shorts. He asked Milo to put the mug of ashes down, took six large shells out of his backpack, and arranged them in a circle around it. After that, he brought out six smooth stones and placed one beside each shell.

The stones had names written on them in marker pen—Lawmaker, Teller, Deputy, Teacher, Joker and Page—so we knew where we had to stand. It felt strange, and wrong, but at the same time it felt right. Duncan had created the Binding; he was the one who knew how it should be ended.

We joined hands and slowly turned towards the left, while Duncan said:

In unwinding, round and round
What we unwind is unwound
What we unbind is unbound
The Binding.

We changed direction and repeated the words, finally coming to a stop and dropping hands. Then Duncan scooped some of the ash out of the tin mug with his shell, picked up his stone and walked slowly into the sea. When he was up to his knees, he scattered the ash on the water and dropped the stone into the middle of it.

Duncan turned and looked at Elspeth, and she copied exactly what he had done. One by one, we all followed him into the water, scattered our ashes and dropped our name stones into the middle of them.

The water was chilly and crystal clear, with hardly any waves. The ashes lay like a film of dust on the surface. We stood there for a while, until our feet were numb with cold, and it was Milo who broke the spell, splashing out to put his shoes on.

I thought Duncan would go away once we'd picked up our shoes because he'd done what he'd come to do, but he hung around. Nobody actually asked him to join in, but when we played knock-the-bottle-off-the-rock, he picked his stones too, and took his turn throwing, though he sat a bit further away, to one side. We didn't invite him, but we didn't stop him either.

It was the same when we played French cricket, and when we went to lie down on the dry sand at the top of the beach, he tagged along too. We were lying in a line with our eyes closed when Elspeth said, 'We're going to see if we can use Anderson Ground for our new den.'

Why was she telling Duncan? Surely he wasn't going to be part of it! But even as I had the thought, I realised that, of course, he was. In a tiny place like this, everyone was part of everything.

'I know a story about Anderson Ground,' said Duncan. 'It's the story of the last and first tree on Morna. I could tell it to you later, if you like.'

We all knew what 'later' meant. It meant when we were all there amongst the gnarled old trees together.

'Shall we go and check it out?' Hamish said, ignoring Duncan but not really ignoring him.

He and Tressa went on ahead, with Milo running at their heels like a happy puppy. Duncan followed a bit behind. He didn't have his stick any more. He'd probably burnt it with all the other things of the Binding.

Elspeth and me didn't stand up straight away, but rolled over on our fronts to watch them make their way up the beach.

'How can you trust him?' I said. 'What if it all starts again after Tressa and me have gone home?'

'It won't. Me and Hamish won't let it. And anyway, I don't think Duncan would want it. I think things just got out of hand, he got carried away, and maybe he frightened himself.'

I didn't believe that for one minute, and I wondered if she really did. I glanced across at her.

'Don't worry,' Elspeth said, seeing the look on my face. 'We'll be in my place, on Anderson Ground, with my mum and dad just across the field, and everything will feel different, with Meggie and Christa joining in.'

'Are you two coming?' Hamish shouted, from the top of the beach.

As we followed them back across the fields to the track, Elspeth told me she wished we weren't leaving at the end of the summer.

'We've still got a couple of weeks,' I said.

'And I suppose that when you go home, we can always Skype and message each other, can't we?'

That reminded me of a joke. I wasn't ready to tell jokes to the whole group again, specially not with Duncan still around, but I told it to her.

'What do you call sheep that live together?'

She looked at me, groans at the ready.

'You call them pen friends!'

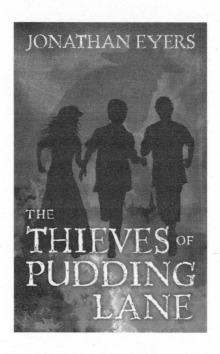

The Thieves of Pudding Lane
Jonathan Eyers

London, 1666.

Orphaned by the Great Plague, Sam is starving on the streets, until the desperate boy joins Uncle Jack's gang of thieves. If Sam is caught by the law, the punishment will be death - and if he crosses Uncle Jack, it could be even worse.

Still, it's a living for Sam and his partner in crime Catherine. Then a blaze at the Pudding Lane bakery runs out of control and, with London burning, the two thieves learn the true evil of Uncle Jack's schemes.

ISBN 978 1 4729 0318 1

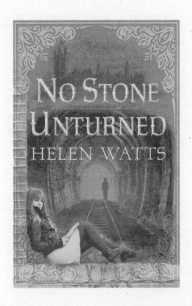

No Stone Unturned
Helen Watts

The past never goes away

Kelly, a Traveller, is isolated and unhappy at her new school.
Until the hot summer day when she meets Ben.

Ben offers to help Kelly with her local history project. It's just schoolwork
- except that the investigation quickly becomes compelling. Strange puzzles
are revealed. The quarry's dark secret is uncovered. Soon the mystery
of the past is spilling into the present - and into Kelly's own life.

Kelly must bring the long-buried truth to light. And she will
leave no stone unturned.

ISBN 978 1 4729 0540 6